JUPITER WINDS

Also by C. J. DARLINGTON

Thicker than Blood
Bound by Guilt
Ties that Bind

JUPITER WINDS

C. J. DARLINGTON

Mountainview Books, LLC

ISBN: 978-0-9891621-3-5 (paperback)
ISBN: 978-0-9891621-4-2 (ebook)

ACKNOWLEDGMENTS

If it weren't for my family, there's no way I could be doing what I'm doing. As always, a big thanks to:

Mom—who's keen editorial insights always make my books stronger. *Jupiter Winds* wouldn't be here without you. Thanks for catching all my mistakes!

Tracy—my biggest fan. Thank you for letting me drone on and on (pun intended!) about my characters and stories. You rock!

James Scott Bell—you've traveled the road before me, and by watching your journey I learn so much. I will always appreciate your advice and encouragement.

Kathy Tyers—for taking the time to offer me valuable feedback on the speculative fiction genre and all its nuances.

Deena Peterson, Beth McComber, and Lori Twichell—beta readers extraordinaire! Thank you, ladies.

Robert Keller—for always being eager to go to the movies. I think all those speculative tales we've watched rubbed off on me! I appreciate your friendship.

My Savior—you've stuck with me through it all.

1

Grey Alexander crouched behind a fat saguaro cactus and tried not to think about getting killed.

"Hear anything, Rin?"

Her younger sister Orinda listened with her auris plug then shook her head. So far, she'd heard nothing but a thundering herd of thirsty zebras. But that didn't mean they were safe.

Grey knelt in the hot, gritty dirt. Flyovers didn't happen often in the Preserve, but with a bounty on the heads of the unconnected, some pilots considered them easy money. And Mazdaar didn't care if the bodies were still breathing or not.

She tapped at her bracelet controller, and the turquoise stone transformed into a grid of thumbnail touchscreens. Running her finger across the grid to activate the ocelli contact lenses in her eyes, Grey focused on a stretch of sage-pocked desert a quarter mile away. They hadn't been able to afford implants for both of them, instead designating Rin as the ears of the mission and Grey as the eyes.

The ocelli immediately brought the area into sharp focus. Along the edge of Grey's vision field, tiny red numbers indicated 8x zoom and F16 aperture. She sometimes imagined she could see the voltage of the invisible electric border fence shimmering in the desert heat.

Grey tapped her wrist again, wishing the lenses could perform x-ray scans. What if she missed a robot drone?

"Looks clear to me," Grey said, giving her sister a thumbs-up. They sprinted across the desert floor, darting around the scattered scrub and ironwood trees. Her heavy pack thumped uncomfortably against her back, making her glad Orinda had the lighter one.

The sisters zeroed in on their target, a sandstone rock they'd strategically placed to mark where they'd dug under the fence last time. As soon as they reached it, Rin tuned in for any sounds of a patrol. Grey waved her hand over the ground. Her DNA registered in the chameleon cloth sensor and an outline appeared in the dirt, revealing a three-foot-square piece of fabric. Able to match the image of any surface and project the picture onto itself, it masked their hole perfectly. Grey had traded a month's worth of food for it.

Quickly jerking the chameleon cloth away and being careful to keep her hand on her side of the fence, she stared at the thick, black wire snaking across the ground above the hole. Grey licked at her cracked lips and slipped out of her pack. Luckily, the fence only emanated an electric force field upward and Mazdaar hadn't bothered to bury the wire more than a few inches.

She shoved her pack under the wire before slowly slithering after it on her stomach. Many had died trying to cross this border, and now she could hear the wire humming with voltage that could kill her too. Halfway across, with the wire only inches from touching her back, she sucked in a breath and caught a mouthful of dust. She suddenly felt trapped, pinned down, and unable to escape.

"You have plenty of room," Rin encouraged her.

She forced her body through the rest of the way and clambered to her feet on the other side of the border, gasping in air. She gave the area one last scan, glad no cameras were installed out here. It was just them and the lizards.

Grey waved for Rin to follow, and her sister didn't hesitate. She slipped under the wire and joined Grey on the other side. Grey repositioned the chameleon cloth, and they were off again at a jog.

This stretch of the border between the Alamo Republic and the North American Wildlife Preserve was always the least patrolled. Only drones traveled this far from the city zones, and the few unconnected people who managed to stay alive in the land of canyons, cacti, and lions didn't want anything to do with Mazdaar.

Still, they could never be too cautious. As far as Mazdaar was concerned, both she and Orinda were outlaws just by being unconnected. The contents of their backpacks alone could send them to the Mars prisons, not to mention their black-market implants and the small, unregistered coilgun Grey wore in a holster around her ankle. It would never be as powerful as any of the laser weapons of Mazdaar, but it would protect them.

Grey huffed a little as they jogged, sweat tickling down her temple. If she and Orinda were to race, Rin would win every time. Thinner, stealthier, and with the grace of a coyote, her fourteen-year-old sister was the only reason Grey had taken these smuggling jobs in the first place. Alone, she might've given up when Mom and Dad disappeared, but Rin gave her a reason to survive.

"Two more miles." Rin was barely breathing hard.

"He said to wait in our usual spot," Grey said. She pulled

out a rag and tried to clean up her dirt-streaked face as they slowed their pace. She didn't want to look like a wild animal when they met up with Jet.

Rin sent a grin her way. "Tired?"

"Nope."

"Liar."

They laughed, but Grey kept aware of her surroundings. They could still be shot on sight.

"Think he'll short us again?"

"Hope not."

"You'll hold your ground?"

Grey nodded.

Rin gave her a sideways glance, and Grey tried not to think about how Rin shouldn't have to be doing this. She hated to see the worry lines etched on her little sister's forehead.

"We'll be okay," Grey said reassuringly. "We always are, right?"

"I will starve before I sell Tram and Trif."

Their two zorses were patiently waiting for them to return from this job alive. Half zebra, half horse, they were smaller and more robust than horses but calmer than zebras. Perfectly suited for life in the Preserve.

"We won't sell them," Grey said, hoping Rin didn't detect her less-than-convincing tone. She didn't want to either, but if it came down to eating another month or parting ways with the animals—she just hoped she wouldn't have to make that choice.

As their destination neared, Grey's adrenaline spiked. "Pay attention, Rin."

Her sister rolled her eyes, and Grey regretted sounding like a scolding parent. She had to remind herself she was Rin's older sister, not her mother. She wished she could've made Rin stay home and leave these missions to her. That's how it began, but as Rin got older she started secretly following her, and she finally decided it was better to have Rin where she could watch her than worry about her sneaking out alone and unarmed.

More saguaro cactus loomed, and a rattler scuttled across their path. The sun beat down on their heads and Grey wished she'd packed more water, but if everything went as planned Jet would have food and drink waiting for them before their transaction.

Grey held up her hand, and they stopped in their tracks as the one-room shack came into view. It was barely standing. Too many years of sun, wind, and bomb tests had eroded the wood planks into splintered, sagging beams.

The sisters stepped up to its lone door. Grey carefully opened it, her lenses instantly adjusting to the darkness. A scorpion crunched under her boot as Rin closed the door behind them. They quickly took up a defensive position, standing back-to-back, ready to see and fight all directions at once. They knew they risked walking into a trap with every one of these missions.

Wisps of sunlight peeked through the battered slats of the shack's back wall, illuminating a million dust particles.

"Just us," Rin said, and Grey breathed easier knowing Rin's auris probably would've alerted them to any drone.

Standing in the center of the room, Grey thunked the warped floorboards with her boot toe three times, paused, and followed up with two more. She smiled when beneath them came an echoing response.

Rin stuck her finger through one of the knotholes, pressing the hidden switch. The floorboards lifted slightly with a click, just enough for them to pull up the trap door and reveal a set of dark stairs. With her lenses, Grey could see what Rin could not—a man's face staring up at them.

He wasn't Jet.

2

Grey instinctively shoved Rin behind her and whipped out her coilgun. She shielded her sister with her own body, training the weapon on the man's face.

"Stay where you are!"

He raised his hands. "It's okay! Jet sent me."

"Prove it."

Rin whispered, "He's alone."

"Tram and Trif," the man said.

Grey zoomed in on his features with the ocelli. The newest generation of drones looked so human it was hard to tell the difference, but she could usually spot one by its eyes. Their pupils didn't react to light and were always dilated, even in direct sunshine.

This man's eyes seemed responsive, and drones rarely spoke with his natural inflection.

"What did you say?"

"Jet told me to tell you 'Tram and Trif.'"

Jet was the only one in the zones who knew the names of their zorses, and they'd figured it would be a safe password. Grey sheathed her gun, making a snap decision to trust this guy. Jet could've confessed the password under duress, but they had a job to do.

She sent a questioning glance in Rin's direction, and her sister nodded her agreement. They descended the stairs into the bunker, closing the trap door carefully behind them. The man turned his back and led them down the corridor lit by dim, old-fashioned halogen lamps.

"I'm sorry if I startled you," he said.

At least a foot taller than Grey and with the shoulders of a body builder, the man was not someone she wanted to have to fight.

"Who are you?" she asked.

He chuckled at the question. "I forgot you aren't connected."

And she'd forgotten to act like she was. Connected people could mentally access information about each other in seconds. They only needed to think a series of cognitive command prompts to activate their permanent implants.

"Please keep that to yourself," Grey snapped.

"My name is Carr."

Rin poked her in the back, and she tried to soften her tone. "Grey. And my sister's Orinda."

"You're awfully young."

"Where's Jet?"

Carr chuckled. "I can see why he uses you."

"We only deal with Jet, so I sincerely hope you're taking us to him."

"Or what?"

Grey tensed at the man's subtle challenge. Yes, she carried a much-coveted gun, but what did Carr conceal beneath that black tunic? He could be hiding an MI pistol, a device shaped like a gun that at full charge was capable of stopping a heart. And since he was probably connected, he could be communicating with anyone even as they walked. They were clearly vulnerable.

"Listen, Carr," Grey tried to sound friendly. "Jet usually meets us at the shack. We're risking a lot here trusting you."

"Understood." Carr paused in front of a door, allowing a face scanner to recognize him. A light on the handle turned green and he opened it, ushering them into another corridor, much brighter than the last. Jet had reassured them that few knew this bunker existed. It had been built to secure government officials who were now long dead. Grey had been dealing with Jet for a few years, but all she knew for sure about him was that he was extremely wealthy and spoke with an elite dialect.

They passed a security guard armed with a thick plasma rifle, and Grey eyed Orinda. If things went badly they had their escape plan, but she hoped it would never come to that. She didn't want to shoot a man.

She also hoped Rin was still listening with her auris and could warn them of danger. Some frequencies were jammed down here, but so far, Rin still seemed to be receiving. With each step deeper into this underground facility, Grey's nerves frayed a little more.

"This way," Carr said, gesturing toward a door marked *Authorized Only*. He reached for the handle as the invisible camera silently scanned his face again. The green light blinked on and Carr opened the door, holding it for them to enter first.

Grey and Rin walked inside, and Carr quickly stepped back out into the hallway, slamming the door behind them. Grey lunged for the handle a second too late. They were locked in.

"Just procedure," Rin reassured her, and Grey composed

herself. Her sister was right. They'd been down halls like this with Jet, and each door always locked behind them. Still, she hated feeling trapped like a lab rat.

"I'm gonna strangle Jet," Grey muttered.

Rin smiled.

They'd never been in this room before, and Grey quickly took it in. A huge, polished conference table made of glass or clear polymer dominated the space, with at least twenty stools surrounding it. Potted plants adorned each corner, probably real but genetically altered to withstand the underground conditions. Along one wall was a stunning painting of the Mazdaar City skyline.

Grey stepped closer to the work of art. Titled "The New Centre of the World," she was mesmerized by the towering skyscrapers sparkling in the artist's rendition of a sunset over the Middle Eastern city. Some of the buildings were two hundred stories high. Most people dreamed of being chosen to live there, but the sight of it caused something inside Grey to churn.

She turned away.

Still wearing their packs, Grey and Rin wandered around the room. The brown carpet would hide their dirty prints and the cool air set to work drying their sweat, but she wished they could freshen up before meeting with Jet.

Rin held her hand to her ear. "He's coming."

"Where?"

Her sister pointed to the opposite wall. There must be a hidden door.

Sure enough, just as Rin pointed to it, the outline of a door became visible. The panel slid aside and Jet walked in, flanked by a female drone with a slightly uneven gait.

"Ladies," Jet said, giving them a bow. His coat, made of a black textile that somehow shimmered in the light, hugged his lean torso then flared at the waist into long, flowing tails behind him.

"You could've warned us you were sending someone else to meet us."

"But I gave him the password, did I not?" With a wave of his hand, Jet ordered the drone to stand against the wall. She obeyed, giving Grey and Rin a piercing look with her iris-less eyes. Grey tried to keep her focus on Jet. Drones never ceased to give her the creeps.

"Not the point." Grey crossed her arms. "It can't happen again or we're through coming here."

Jet laughed. "Are you now?"

For the second time that day Grey got the feeling their bargaining power was disintegrating. He never discussed how many other scouts he had working for him, but she guessed they weren't the only ones. What, except his past friendship with their parents, was to keep Jet from ripping their packs away and taking their merchandise without even paying?

The hidden door opened once more and a tall man dressed in a blue chef's uniform entered carrying a tray full of food that immediately sent Grey's stomach growling.

Setting the tray on the table, the man placed two square cups beside it and poured steaming coffee into them from a black pot. Grey's annoyance melted just a little. The coffee smelled fantastic. No one outside the zones could afford the beans.

Silently, the man set out the rest of the spread, and Rin honed in on the colorful plate of vegetables they'd never be able to grow in the Preserve's climate. The feast included bright-red peppers, succulent tomatoes, lettuce, and herbs neither of them had enjoyed anywhere else. Grey knew Jet was buttering them up quite literally with the food, but she'd decided from the beginning to relish everything they could on a mission. Who knew the next time they'd get to savor real vegetables or pastries made from chocolate?

"Sit down and enjoy please," Jet said, the lights reflecting off his black hair. Jet black some would say, thus his nickname. She wasn't entirely sure it was real.

Rin and Grey slipped out of their packs, keeping them close at their sides. The exchange would come later. First they would eat, and thankfully Jet let them. They tried not to look as hungry as they were, but it was hard not to devour every last morsel. Jet kept busy talking into the air, probably on a conference call with men and women only he could see.

She watched him in her peripheral vision field. She'd heard he was ten years her senior, but his Asian features made him appear younger. In different garb, he could've been mistaken for a Samurai warrior.

"Shall I have them pack you a box?" Jet asked like he always did when Grey and Rin's consumption slowed. They both nodded, glad he didn't make them ask. They never allowed themselves to fill up so much that they wouldn't be able to run later, which meant not eating nearly what their empty stomachs demanded. Coming home safely from a meeting with Jet always meant good food for at least a week.

The cuisine specialist who'd brought the tray appeared again, carefully stacking their plates and the leftover food. When he left, Jet got down to business.

He leaned forward across the table. "I assume you've been successful?"

Grey unzipped her pack, removing a hard, silver case. Made from an alloy that could withstand radiation and even redflare lasers, Grey had bartered for it when she was thirteen. Pressing her thumb to the fingerprint reader on its side, the box unlocked with a click, and she turned it around for Jet to see.

Nestled in the middle of the box were three of the most

valuable items she'd ever smuggled into the Alamo Republic. Jet's slight gasp confirmed he agreed.

"Where did . . ." Jet waved a hand. "Never mind. It doesn't matter. You got them."

Carefully lifting one of the treasures out of the box, Grey turned it around and marveled that she was actually holding something people might kill for.

"A real, live book," Grey said, handing it to Jet.

"Impressive, ladies." He took it from her, opening the paper covers of *Apology* by Plato.

When Mazdaar took over the infrastructure of the Americas, physical books of all kinds were officially banned, and Mazdaar permanently deleted every electronic book that hadn't been published with their own imprint. Under threat of imprisonment, most citizens finally did surrender their books, but some fled to the wilderness, taking their volumes into hiding with them.

These weren't the first books they'd sold to Jet, but it had taken Grey and Rin six weeks and hundreds of grueling miles of scouting to locate these three, and they'd had to buy them with every remaining piece of silver they'd saved.

"Let me see the others." Jet extended his hand to Grey, but she only stared at it.

"First, our payment," Grey said.

With a dramatic flourish, Jet nodded but said, "And my feast wasn't enough?"

It was a game he liked to play that luckily Grey recognized for what it was. What had first unnerved her and almost made her forget the arrangement entirely felt now like just an irritating waste of their time.

Jet snapped his fingers, and the drone stepped up to the table. Reaching into her uniform pocket, she deposited a small felt pouch on the clear table.

Grey picked it up, careful not to touch the drone's metallic hand, and counted the silver coins inside. Currency of any kind was illegal. Now with a scan of a palm, the cost of anything could be deducted from your official Mazdaar account. Try to use anything else and you'd end up in an interrogation room.

Rin removed a safe box from her pack, setting it on the table as well. She unlocked it and slid it toward Jet, and the contents immediately made Jet smile. The box was packed with cigarettes, a commodity banned even before books. Each "smoke stick" as Grey liked to call them would be worth at least a day's wages.

Jet gave them another bow. "I am satisfied."

Grey carefully counted their payment while Jet and the drone unpacked the cigarettes into a box of their own. She often wondered who would buy them in cities where no-smoking laws threatened capital punishment. Maybe Jet sold them to underground clubs or to some of the government officials who had no trouble breaking the laws they enforced on others. She really didn't care. Not as long as they had their agreed payment.

Except Jet had tried to short them. Again.

Grey slammed the silver onto the table. "You're two hundred grams short."

Jet lifted a cigarette and sniffed it long and hard. "Quality's mediocre."

"It's the best there is."

"I like better."

She crossed her arms. Rin gave her a worried look. Who did they think they were, two girls trying to make a deal with a man like Jet? With a wave of his hand he could probably have them both arrested and handed over to Mazdaar. But they'd been taking care of themselves for five years and had learned how to do business, and Grey wasn't going to let this slide.

She focused on Jet but was keenly aware of the drone standing beside him. They'd even gone to the trouble of wrinkling her bioskin around the eyes where crow's feet would normally appear. What programming had they given this series? Late models could effectively restrain and immobilize the strongest human.

Jet closed his cigarette box with a sigh. "I have paid you what your product is worth."

"Which is not what we agreed."

He waved his hand at the drone, and she slowly turned her head to stare at Grey like she was sizing her up. The cuisine specialist returned, carrying their food packs. He pushed them across the glass table toward Grey and Rin with a smile. They were vacuum sealed and temperature regulated to keep from spoiling under the hottest of conditions.

Grey placed the bundles in her pack and slipped the load onto her shoulders. With a nod to Rin, whose forehead still scrunched with concern, Grey led the way to the door through which they'd entered. "Unlock it."

For the longest moment nothing happened, but then the light turned green, and the two girls left the room.

"We will speak again," Jet said to their backs.

Out in the hallway, escorted by Carr who'd apparently been waiting for them, Grey muttered, "Not likely."

3

Grey's pulse quickened with every step down the corridor. They had to get out of here. She'd stood up to Jet before, but somehow this was different. He seemed bolder than ever, and never had a drone looked at her like that.

She could feel tension radiating off Rin walking beside her, but neither of them allowed their movements to give away their fear. Not even when they were marching down the bunker's exterior tunnel.

Grey and Rin quickly ascended the stairs and climbed up into the shack. The trap door sunk back into the floor, locking with a final click. Grey sighed, pushing the unruly strands of hair that had escaped her ponytail behind her ears.

"How can he do that?" Rin looked ready to cry.

Grey peeked out the cracks of the bowed wooden slats for any sign of trouble outside. The sun was dropping quickly. They needed to hurry to be home before dark.

Nothing stirred except a vulture riding the thermal winds.

"Let's go," Grey said.

"But it's not fair."

Grey grabbed Rin by the shoulders. She'd learned how to mask her feelings for Rin's sake early on, but no matter how hard Rin tried, her youthful inexperience always shone through.

She patted her sister once on her freckled cheek. "Nothing's fair. That's our life."

"What about—"

"Rin, we have to get home."

"Will he let us get home?"

That was the big question, really. They didn't know the full extent of Jet's influence. He definitely had some major resources, but was he in cahoots with Mazdaar?

"Focus on Tram and Trif. They're waiting for us."

Grey and Rin stepped from the shack, squinting in the daylight. As they walked, Grey scanned every cactus and scrub with her lenses. Anything could be hiding out here.

"What should we do about Jet?"

She increased her pace, Rin right behind her. She'd never lied to her little sister, but there were plenty of things she hadn't shared. Like how much danger they were in on these jobs.

A faint *snap* made her freeze.

"Grey?" Rin whispered

She held up her hand. The ocelli wouldn't be much help if something snuck up behind them.

"Do you hear something?"

Rin came to stand beside her, a flash of fear in her eyes. "I turned it off while we were eating. Grey, I'm—"

She ripped her pistol from its holster just as a drone twice her size pushed through the scrub. One glance at its tan uniform and the red, seven-pointed-star emblem on its chest pegged it as a Mazdaar border patroller, complete with a hand-held derma-ray aimed right at them.

"Identify," he ordered.

Grey clenched her jaw. The weapon's high-powered waves excited the atoms in a person's skin, making it feel like it was on fire. She had about three seconds before he would confirm they weren't connected and detain them.

The drone's eyes blinked, and she was startled at how human its male face looked.

It's just a machine. Just a machine.

Without warning, the drone turned on Rin and shot her point blank with the derma-ray. Her sister screamed and fell, writhing in the sand.

Grey fired her own weapon at the drone's chest, wincing at the deafening sound and the kickback from the coilgun. If the drone hadn't already called for reinforcements, that blast surely would. The drone stumbled backward. Its derma-ray dropped to the desert floor, and Grey pulled Rin to her feet. "You okay?"

Rin nodded. Though excruciating, a derma-ray's effects instantly disappeared the moment the weapon was directed elsewhere.

"Then run!"

She pushed her sister forward as the drone let out a low moan behind them. Grey swung around. The patroller clutched its chest with a gloved hand, crimson blood oozing through his tunic. She suddenly felt nauseous.

Drones didn't have blood.

"Grey!"

"No, no, no . . ." She started toward him, but Rin latched onto her arm and jerked her away.

"I thought he was—"

"We have to go now!"

She forced herself to follow her sister, glancing over her shoulder at the bleeding man who was not a drone at all. She'd aimed for his heart. He could die, but if she stayed to help him she and Rin would be dead as well.

"There's nothing you can do," Rin said. "Don't think about it. Not now."

Grey finally ran too, stuffing her horror as best she could. They had to survive. She couldn't fail her sister now.

Twenty minutes later, they reached the fence and repeated the process of slipping under the wire in reverse. Grey took the chameleon cloth with them. They wouldn't be able to return this way again.

It was almost an hour of painstaking travel, sneaking from cactus to cactus before they reached the rim rocks. The massive sandstone boulders overlooked the desert, providing a natural cover that allowed them to finally let down their guard. Mazdaar wouldn't bother sending patrols out here.

Slipping through a cleft in the rock just large enough for a human to pass through, Grey and Rin walked into a small clearing that was completely surrounded by the boulders towering hundreds of feet above them. They paused to watch and listen with their respective devices, and Rin gave her a small nod.

"It's my fault," Rin said. "I should've been listening. I—"

Grey shook her head. "It wasn't."

"I was sure he was a drone too."

"Since when do they send *men* on border patrol?" Grey cursed. She had to remind herself he'd shot Rin first and would've turned them in to officials who would do far worse. But still—she'd never shot a human before.

Two whinnies greeted them, and Rin bounded over to Tram and Trif who were contentedly munching on the wildflowers and prickly pear cactus growing in the clearing. The coats of the zorses were a light brown, but their faint, telltale black stripes spoke of their zebra heritage.

Rin threw her arms around the neck of the smaller zorse, Trif, and Grey had to smile at her sister's affection for the animal.

"Told you we'd be back," Rin said into Trif's neck as he nuzzled her shoulder.

Grey watched them for a moment. Around the zorse Rin was just a girl again, and Grey realized she'd do anything in her power to keep these pets for her sister. Which wasn't going to be easy, since she'd made up her mind about Jet.

"Hey there, boy," Grey approached Tram who, though the larger of the two, was less dominant and usually hung back. He allowed Grey to stroke his neck, and they enjoyed each other's company in silence. But the slowly-darkening sky reminded Grey their mission wasn't yet complete.

"Time to saddle up," she called to Rin, and they set to work preparing the animals for the ride home. The girls stripped out of their dirty, sweat-caked camo, stuffing the clothes into their saddle bags with the food packs. They compressed the backpacks, tied them behind the saddles, and quickly dressed in cooler, loose-fitting tunics and canvas pants.

Grey gave Rin a leg up onto Trif then climbed into Tram's saddle and led the way out down the only other path between the boulders. There was just enough room here for them to ride single-file without scraping their legs against the rock.

They rode silently for the next two hours across the desert terrain. The blue sky darkened to a deep purple, leaving only the tops of the distant mountains still glowing in sunlight. Grey took in a deep breath of the sage-scented air, allowing herself to close her eyes for just a second. She'd done what she had to.

As they neared home, pine trees and scrub oak gave them better cover. The air cooled and blew across their faces as night fell. With a tap to her bracelet controller, Grey zeroed the ocelli in on the elephant-sized boulder with the flat top, searching for any signs that their location had been compromised. Was there a camouflaged drone hiding behind one of those trees?

Grey stared at the boulder that meant their journey was almost over. Her whole body ached, and she couldn't wait to take a cool, refreshing bath.

"We're done with Jet," Grey said.

"What? But how can we survive without—"

"We will," Grey said. "Somehow we will, Rin."

She didn't tell her sister she had no idea how. For the past five years they'd lived this life, sometimes bringing prohibited goods to people like Jet, other times smuggling stuff out of the Amarillo Zone for the few people in the Preserve who could pay. It had become familiar, and they were good at it.

"If only Mom and Dad . . ."

Grey nodded.

They didn't talk about them often, but the loss of their parents still cut deeply. Grey had been twelve, Rin three years younger. One day Mom and Dad went out on what was supposed to be a week-long hunting trip and never came back. If it hadn't been for the food and water their parents had stockpiled and their neighbor Mrs. March's kind help, the girls would've starved. For years Grey held on to the hope that someday they'd come walking back home with some grand story to tell. She'd never admit it to Rin, but Grey now realized that had just been the desperate dream of an orphaned daughter.

Tram and Trif sped up now. As hidden as the compound was, the zorses knew exactly where they were. Fresh water and their dinner awaited them.

Loosening her reins, Grey let Tram pick the path across the rough terrain. At the boulder, the sisters dismounted, leading the zorses into the stand of gnarled scrub oak that was their front yard. They waited, listening, watching. The night's first and brightest star, Vega, glistened above them. Finally, Grey approached the boulder.

Be my rock of refuge, to which I can always go.

She wished the snippet of a verse her mother used to recite didn't always spring to mind when she saw the boulder. As a little girl she'd listened to Mom's memorized Scripture lines, and they always seemed to pop up at the most inopportune times.

To the untrained eye, the rock was a natural part of the landscape, a fixture for hundreds of years. Which was exactly how it was designed to look. In reality, the man-made hunk of gypsum concealed the entrance to their subterranean home.

During the day, they usually let the zorses roam outside since they were trained to always return. If a flyby spotted Tram and Trif, their presence wouldn't give Rin and Grey away. Herds of horse, zebra, and zorse roamed the Preserve, which gave the girls comfort. If anything ever happened to them, Tram and Trif could eventually find their way into one of the herds.

Rin unlocked the door in the rock using her thumbprint. The gray metal panel slid open, and they led the zorses down the ramp, inside to the second security door. Automatic lights switched on after the first door closed behind them. Powered by the hidden solar panels that lined the ridge, they provided more than enough illumination for the silo.

Circular and about a thousand feet square, they'd converted the top room of the dwelling into comfortable living quarters for the animals. Half the cement floor was covered with pine needles on bartered rubber mats that had to be cleaned daily, but neither of them minded the chore. The ceiling was tallest here, over twenty feet, and air vents to the surface helped keep the smell down. Drains in the floor helped with cleanup too.

Once Tram and Trif were settled and their tack secured and checked for wear, Grey and Rin made their way to the door against the far wall, stomping their feet on the scrap of rug they kept there to clean their boots. They passed through and headed down the stairs with heavy steps.

Finally, they were home.

So, what was your favorite?" Rin was perched on a step halfway up the main level's spiral staircase, her legs dangling in the space below.

Grey put the last packet of food away in the cooling box. Years ago, this place had been a missile silo. Eventually abandoned, it had been converted and retrofitted years later by some millionaire who'd hope to make it a second home. He'd probably been killed by one of the nukes during the War, because it was never completed.

"The cheese," she finally responded, knowing Rin was trying to get her mind off the patroller she'd shot.

"I could've fainted when I saw those strawberries."

Imitating Jet, Grey withdrew the pack containing the fresh fruit with a flourish and brought it over to Rin. "My lady." She bowed and presented it to her sister. "Your delicacy awaits."

Giggling, Rin climbed down the steps, and together they polished them off. On the day of a mission they allowed themselves to eat as much as their stomachs could hold once they were home safe and sound. It would be back to careful rations the rest of the month.

"I wish you didn't have to go tomorrow," Rin said after they were washed up, had removed and plugged in their implants, and were lounging in the low, plush chairs along the wall.

"Shh. Don't think about that." Grey mussed her sister's short hair and swiped her bracelet controller. It was also programmed to control some of the silo's equipment.

She cued up Rin's favorite movie, a story about a girl who tames wild tigers. They'd watched it dozens of times, but their cache of films was limited to those their grandparents had managed to collect before the last of the American servers was destroyed by the sweeping Mazdaar army.

With the press of her finger the lights dimmed, and the opening scene of the movie materialized in front of them in holographic 3D. By the end credits Grey could barely keep her eyes open, even as Rin babbled on about finding an orphan tiger cub and raising it herself someday.

"In your dreams," Grey said.

Leaving the lights off, they climbed down the stairs to their sleeping level. The circular room was way too big for two girls, but they were used to the empty space by now and fell into their side-by-side beds.

Grey listened to Rin's breathing slow. She kept her own eyes open.

"Grey?"

"Yeah."

"Can you pray?"

"What?"

"That everything'll be okay?"

She sighed, crossing her arms on her chest. She couldn't

remember the last time she'd prayed. It was before Mom and Dad left; she knew that.

"Go to sleep, kid."

A few minutes later, a soft little snore came from Rin's bed, and Grey didn't worry about waking her sister as she crept down the stairs. Rin didn't often visit the lowest level in their silo, but Grey did when she couldn't sleep.

Dad's workshop was exactly as he'd left it. Along the perimeter of the room a ledge four feet wide extended, littered with machinery, parts, and tools she couldn't identify. Some of them dated back to when the U.S. still existed. Dad used to tell them stories about the freedom people enjoyed back then and how they would travel around in vehicles they piloted themselves.

Grey had tried to make sense of the clutter without much success. She knew Dad would've catalogued everything, but his controller had disappeared with him.

She picked up a screwdriver and closed her eyes, trying to picture his huge hands and how they'd enveloped this tool. With every month that passed, her memories faded. She squeezed the archaic instrument, swallowing against the lump trying to form in her throat, and carefully placed it back on the shelf.

Pressing her thumb into a blank space on the wall, a three-by-six-foot section of it disappeared, presenting her with an opening she walked through. The lights in this tubular corridor with metallic walls were dim and far apart. A musty smell met her nose, and she noticed a puddle in the corner. She'd have to check into that.

Grey stepped out onto a metal grated catwalk, letting the door swoosh shut. Total blackness surrounded her like a coat, and she stood for a moment picturing her father standing here like this when they were in bed. She remembered the first time

Dad brought her down here, when her young mind couldn't grasp what she saw.

She felt for the catwalk railing and the control box mounted to its frame. She knew which button to push by feel. Pressing it, the floodlights snapped on and spread light through the cavern. Grey stood in awe just like she had the first time.

The space stretched above her more than a hundred feet. She steadied herself against the railing and peered down. Below was where the deadly missiles had been kept. They'd long ago been removed, and Dad had told her most of these silos had stood abandoned and forgotten for decades.

But he never did explain the reason why sitting in their silo was an enormous, sleek, blue cosmoship.

Grey was up before the sun. She hated leaving Rin alone, but one person could hide better than two out here, and she knew the girl could take care of herself. She'd probably spend the day with Tram and Trif, trying to teach them some silly trick she saw in the movie last night.

When it was light enough to see where she was going, Grey set out with her coilgun and a canteen of water, wishing she could wear the ocelli lenses every time she traveled the Preserve. But her natural vision would deteriorate with their overuse, and she wasn't sure how long the lenses themselves would last either. She tried to use them only for important missions.

Stuffed in her pocket were some of the silver coins Jet had given them. As she walked, she thought about how different this land must've looked before Mazdaar took over. It was hard to picture. The old towns, the homes—all were rubble or abandoned. The people were either dead or relocated to the city-zones within the Alamo Republic and the Cascade Territory on the coast, or in the case of a select few, Mazdaar City.

The new city-zones of North America were strictly controlled by Mazdaar, and she'd heard it was the same in Europe and Africa. The Yien Dynasty, while less powerful than Mazdaar, still controlled Asia and manufactured the technology Mazdaar needed. Grey didn't know much about Yien's people, but she did know about Mazdaar.

Few ever traveled outside the city zones. Only elite government officials and billionaire socialites were taken on scheduled Mazdaar safari hunts in the Preserve. After all, that's what the North American Wildlife Preserve was originally created to be—a tourist attraction for the rich and powerful who got tired of traveling to Mars.

While the Preserve was being built and the wilderness recovered from radiation poisoning, most people resumed life in their new, high-tech cities. But there were some, like her family, who had ducked under the radar outside the zones.

Grey took in a deep breath of the arid air. Scattered among the rocks, canyons, and reintroduced wild animals, enough unconnected people subsisted to make trade viable. You just had to know where to look for them.

She walked five miles before she came to Mrs. March's cave, and Grey made sure to stay in full view. She didn't want to startle her neighbor.

"Mrs. March? It's me, Grey," she said in a normal volume.

Waiting patiently, Grey listened for any sounds that didn't belong but only heard a hawk screeching somewhere far away.

"I was getting worried."

Grey started at the voice coming from behind her. Mrs. March could sneak up on a lynx.

The white-haired woman smiled. Dressed in thread-worn jeans and a white tunic with frills and puffy sleeves, Mrs. March was all bones and sinew but gave fierce hugs.

Grey remained in her embrace longer than usual. Mrs. March had looked after them when Mom and Dad disappeared, always making sure they had supplies and teaching them how to survive. She was the only person Grey knew who could remember life before Mazdaar connected the world.

She was also the oldest person Grey had ever seen. The woman never revealed her exact age, but she had to be in her eighties. Without the surgeries and supplements most people resorted to at half her years, she actually looked it too.

"What's wrong?" Mrs. March held her at arm's length.

Grey hadn't intended to speak of the border patroller, but her neighbor could read her like her mom used to. She told Mrs. March what happened.

"I think I killed him."

Mrs. March studied her with clear, green eyes. "You were protecting your family."

She swallowed hard. "He shot Rin."

"And would've done worse if you hadn't stopped him."

Grey turned toward the cleft in the rock which led to Mrs. March's home. The woman's technology was older than theirs, but she still had a blast-proof entrance that opened via fingerprint and cameras spaced strategically outside.

Her receivers were what made her the go-to woman for news of Mazdaar. Every day she listened in on secure frequencies she'd managed to hack, gathering intelligence from the zones.

Everyone out here was an outcast, but for how long could they remain? No one knew, but Mrs. March's updates helped. Rumors cropped up every few months about Mazdaar sending out raiding parties to hunt down the unconnected and rid the Preserve of them once and for all. They all hoped she would pick up on enough chatter before something like that happened.

"What have you been hearing?" Grey asked as they walked into the cave. She needed to talk about something else.

The room was smaller than any of the floors of their silo, and Mrs. March had decorated with artifacts she'd collected over the years. A giraffe-pelt rug covered the stone floor.

"Things are afoot." Mrs. March gestured for her to sit on one of the stumps she'd positioned around a rock in the center of the room.

"We had a little trouble with Jet too." Grey shared how Jet had shorted them. "Why would he do that again? You said we could trust him."

"How much did he pay you?"

"Two hundred grams less than our deal."

Mrs. March's pale eyebrows shot up. "That much less?"

"I'm not sure if we can go back."

"We'll work it out." Mrs. March brought over some of her cactus tea that Grey couldn't stand but Mrs. March thought she loved. The teacups were made of antique ceramic, though each one had chips along the edges and their saucers had disappeared long ago.

"I hope so."

"You can sell to others."

Grey slipped out of her pack, deciding not to remind Mrs. March that Jet was their best customer.

"How is Orinda?"

"She's spoiling Tram and Trif." Grey pulled the coins from her pocket. "And I brought your money."

"Thank you."

Even though Jet had cut them short, she always gave her sources exactly what she owed them. For local traders, she paid half up front and the rest after a transaction was completed. They'd sold several of Mrs. March's books in the past to Jet, including her copy of *The Theory of Relativity* yesterday. As Grey handed over the coins, Mrs. March wrapped her fingers around Grey's hand, pushing it away.

"Mrs. March . . ."

"You girls need this more than I do."

"We're fine. You—"

"Just come see me again sometime soon. That's payment enough."

Grey slowly returned the money to her pocket. "I'll do you one better. Why don't you come up to our place? Jet gave us some great food this time."

Mrs. March smiled. "Deal."

"What chatter have you been hearing?"

"Do you know the name Evangeline Yurkutz?"

Grey could not forget the one hologram she had seen of the Mazdaar official. Her spiked black hair with the frosty tips and her yellow eyes gave her an intensity that reminded Grey of a cougar.

"Mazdaar military general, right?"

"And leader of the High Council."

Grey grimaced. She had heard nothing good about the Mazdaar High Council. Anyone who ended up in front of them usually didn't come back.

"Steer clear of anything to do with General Yurkutz," Mrs. March said.

"Not a problem," Grey said.

"She's been making some waves, and we're keeping a careful watch on her movements."

"Waves? What do you mean?"

"Let's just say she's a danger to all of us." Mrs. March sighed. "There's also been lots of talk about Jupiter."

That surprised Grey. Mars used to be the place to be. Once they figured out how to create the atmosphere by planting trees and installing oxygen generators, travel to the planet became affordable even for the middle class. Jupiter must be the next planet in Mazdaar's sites.

"I thought it was still uninhabitable." Grey took a sip of the cactus tea and had to force herself not to grimace. The cocktail of juices with a little pulp was so bitter she could barely swallow. She had no idea how Mrs. March could down the stuff like water.

Mrs. March fell silent, and Grey didn't press her to speak. She was used to her neighbor's pauses. They usually meant she was in deep thought and her next words could be nuggets of wisdom.

"That's what we were told." Mrs. March's voice was low.

Grey set down her cup, hoping Mrs. March wouldn't notice it was still full. Maybe she could pour a little out somewhere when she wasn't looking.

Leaning over the table, Mrs. March met her eyes. "Grey, you're old enough now to hear some of this. You don't believe everything Mazdaar says, right?"

"I wouldn't be here if I did."

"There's a lot they *don't* say."

"I have never trusted them, Mrs. March."

"What if I told you that not only is Jupiter habitable, but there are people living there right now?"

Grey thought for a moment. She'd read in one of the books they'd traded to Jet that it was a scientific fact that the Eye of Jupiter was a huge storm that never calmed, but years ago when they sent a probe down through it they discovered that underneath the storm was level land, solid enough to support a shuttle landing. But habitable? Men needed space suits to survive on the surface as far as she knew.

"Who was the first man on Jupiter?" Mrs. March quizzed.

"Lars Nolan."

"Ah." Mrs. March held up her finger. "That's the official

record, yes. In reality, the first man on Jupiter was actually a convict named Samuel Bradford."

"A convict?"

"There were people who set foot on the planet years before Lars."

Grey wasn't sure if she could believe everything this quirky lady said, but it didn't surprise her that the Mazdaar official record wasn't accurate.

"But have any of you young people heard of them?" Mrs. March nodded her head to emphasize the point. "No, of course not."

"So how do *you* know?"

Mrs. March's eyes widened. It was almost as if she'd been talking to herself and just noticed Grey sitting at her kitchen table. She stared at her.

"Mrs. March?"

"I know," the old woman said with a sigh, "because I've been there."

5

Grey laughed, but Mrs. March didn't.

"You're serious?"

"Very."

She studied the woman's weathered face, noticing the small hole in her nostril from an old piercing. She almost laughed again, picturing Mrs. March with a nose ring, but she stopped herself. There was no jest in the woman's green eyes.

"And I'm worried about you girls." Mrs. March took a sip from her teacup.

Grey stared into her own cup. She wished she could say something to assuage her neighbor's concern, but they both knew every time she and Rin ran a mission they risked capture. She forced herself to take a sip. "You've really been to Jupiter?"

"I was a pilot for Mazdaar many years ago. I flew those convicts in."

"Wow."

Mrs. March was as tall as Grey but willowy like Rin. Her clothes hung loosely on her thin frame. She didn't look anything like what Grey imagined a pilot should be.

Mrs. March smiled. "I know that's hard to fathom."

"A little."

"It's time we all started thinking about Jupiter. Grey, things are changing. Fast. I don't want you girls caught in the crossfire." Concern etched in Mrs. March's age-spotted face. "There's a great deal you don't know."

"So tell me."

"I will. But Rin should hear it too. Why don't I come over tomorrow, and we can all discuss this more?" Mrs. March poured herself more tea. "And I could do with some of Jet's delicacies."

Grey stood up, shaking her head. "It'll take more than a few strawberries to wrap my mind around all this."

"I promise it'll make more sense tomorrow." Mrs. March walked her outside. "But in the meantime, please be cautious."

"I always am."

Grey's next stop was to the dealer who made the cigarettes. He wasn't nearly as friendly as Mrs. March. Grey had also paid him half of his cut when she picked up the order, and she was here to give him the rest. She made sure her coilgun was safely strapped to the side of her ankle as she approached his dwelling. It was inconspicuous there under her pant leg, and she knew Kildare Rooley would be looking. In his line of work, he didn't trust anyone.

The sun was high in the sky when she approached his property four miles from Mrs. March's cave. Nestled in the side of Devil's Bluff and hidden by a stand of scrub oak, the entrance to his "farm" was a primitive wooden door. The place had once been a gold mine, long ago abandoned. Kildare hoped no one would imagine that someone lived in such a dilapidated place.

At the first growl, Grey stopped in her tracks.

She'd almost reached the oaks, and she knew Kildare would be watching her every move with his surveillance cameras. The second growl was closer, and she could almost feel the deep rumble as she simultaneously picked up its pungent scent.

"It's Grey," she called. Kildare had chewed her out last visit for calling too loudly, but she wanted to make sure he knew she wasn't an intruder.

Something rustled in the trees, and she felt chill bumps on the back of her neck.

Come on, come on!

She knew the only reason Kildare dealt with her at all was because she never showed her fear. But that didn't mean she never felt it.

A twig snapped.

She focused on the movement only ten feet from her. A flash of orange-and-black fur slipped from view. Then she saw it. She could smell the animal's rank, iron-tinged breath.

"I've got your payment," she said just above a whisper. He'd probably heard her the first time, but she couldn't just stand here being stalked.

Leaves rustled again, and the tiger's face pushed through the brush. His teeth were the size of her fingers, his body bigger than Tram or Trif. A second tiger appeared, panting in the heat. Both of them stared right at her, eyes intent on their prey. She'd heard they'd eaten off at least one man's arm in the past.

The huge tigers sat on their haunches, waiting for her next move. She didn't dare turn her back on them or run. Kildare had them trained to wait for his commands in their ear implants, but Grey couldn't look at those massive jaws without feeling like tiger bait.

She saw rather than heard when Kildare finally called off the cats by the twitch of their ears. They slunk off into the brush again, and a barefoot young boy appeared, waving for Grey to follow him. She recognized him as Jonah, Kildare's only son.

She and Jonah passed through the first doorway into almost complete darkness—at least it seemed that way at first, coming straight from the blistering sunshine. Grey followed the sound of Jonah's footsteps until her eyes adjusted and his energetic form took shape again. Torches along the stone wall illuminated their path.

Jonah turned a corner and they faced another wooden entry, this one smooth and polished. He pulled it open using all his body weight. Grey stayed close as they entered the widening cavern, and now she had to squint in the sudden brightness.

Hanging from the ceiling, gigantic UV lights shone over rows of broad-leafed green plants. Workers dressed in white body suits with protective glasses and face shields were busy tilling in between the rows.

Grey shielded her eyes and could just make out Kildare walking toward them. He was the only one here not wearing white and instead wore a dark blue jumpsuit. A Panama straw hat shielded most of his face. She'd never seen the man smile.

"You're late," Kildare said.

"I'm here."

Kildare waved his son on to other matters, and the boy scampered off.

"You're still late."

Grey pulled the carefully-counted coins from her tunic

pocket and handed them to the man. Bringing the silver close to his face, Kildare made sure to count it himself. He jerked a thumb toward his indoor field. "New crop's almost ready."

"Same price?"

"Maybe."

Which meant he'd be raising it again. Jet would not be pleased. If she ever worked with Jet again, that is. She decided now wasn't the time to negotiate. Rin would worry if she wasn't home before dark.

She turned to leave, but Kildare cleared his throat. Grey knew better than to proceed. With her back to him, she waited.

"Be careful," he said.

Grey twisted around to see his face, but he'd already disappeared back into his domain of tobacco and artificial sunshine.

Grey was a mile from home when she sensed something was wrong. Growing up as they had, she'd learned early on to trust her gut. It could save their lives. She paused beside a boulder, scanning the landscape and wishing once more she had brought the ocelli.

Far in the distance, she thought she spotted a tower of giraffes gathered around one of the few natural watering holes. Closer by, a lioness sprawled beneath an oak tree, panting and waiting for nightfall. A few white cirrus clouds streaked through the sky, but she saw nothing to set her on edge. Nothing to confirm her hunch.

The heavens declare the glory of God; the skies proclaim the work of his hands.

Oh, please. Not now.

Grey resumed walking, flinging the quote from her mind. She needed to concentrate. Carefully, slowly, she placed one foot in front of the other and continued to scan her surroundings.

If a wild animal was following her, it was possible she wouldn't see it in time to react.

Rock clacked against rock, and Grey spun around, holding her breath so she could listen. If only she had Rin's auris.

Reaching for her ankle, she unbuckled the gun and waited. But as the sun dipped closer to the line of hazy mountains in the West, there was nothing but a roadrunner trilling from far away and a lizard crawling across the dirt. The wind blew through the branches of the scrub oak, a sound she normally enjoyed. She must just be on edge or overly tired. What she really needed was a cool bath and some of Jet's delicious leftovers.

Her mouth watered thinking about biting into one of the chocolate apple crisps, and Grey re-holstered the gun and pushed forward toward their silo entrance.

Out of nowhere, a catchship rose over the ridge. Completely silent, it sent stinging dust flying into Grey's eyes. She held up her sleeve to ward off the debris, glancing in the direction of home. If she ran, she could make it. In a few mad sprints she'd be safely locked behind their steel door, Tram and Trif looking up at her from their dinner wondering what all the commotion was about.

But Grey saw the Mazdaar star insignia on the ship's side, and she realized that by running she'd be leading the craft straight to their home.

Straight to Rin.

Grey covered her face with her hand and turned away from the hidden entry. Tears filled her eyes as much from the gritty dirt as from the understanding that her worst fears were coming to pass.

Stay inside, Rin. Stay inside!

If her sister came running out here, they would both be captured. At least this way she could keep her sister safe. Rin would figure out a way to survive without her. Mrs. March would take her in if need be.

The catchship hovered ten feet off the ground in front of her and a deep voice boomed, "Grey Alexander, you are ordered to kneel and place your hands on your head. If you do not comply, we will open fire."

She closed her eyes, falling to her knees as the ship dropped the rest of the way to the ground. The moment it thudded on the desert floor and Grey felt the impact through her body, an opening appeared and two armed metallic drones—they hadn't bothered covering these with bioskin—in the Mazdaar silver-and-green uniform marched toward her. One of them snapped thin wire restraints on her wrists that she knew were made of unbreakable titanium. If someone tried too hard to remove them they'd dig through muscle and bone. The other drone ripped her pant leg and tore her gun away.

Icy, metallic fingers grabbed her arms and raised her to her feet, shoving her toward the gaping hole in the catchship. Grey longed to look back and call out to her sister, to tell her to be brave and strong and to trust no one but Mrs. March. She closed her eyes as they shoved her inside the ship.

I love you, Rin.

The huge hatch zipped closed behind her, and she felt the ship rise under her feet with a sickening lurch even as the drones pushed her into a seat along the wall.

The reality of what was happening hit her like the frigid air inside the dark ship. Surrounded by black metal and huge support beams, there was no color other than the drones' uniforms. Grey's stomach dropped as the ship flew upward and then quickly leveled. Ships like these could reach the Plano city zone, the capital of the Alamo Republic, within minutes.

But the minutes ticked by, and the drones stood silent guard over her. If this was a Mazdaar catchship, wouldn't they take her straight to the capital base? And wouldn't they have arrived by now? She knew asking questions of the drones would be futile as they were probably programmed only to make the grab.

After at least an hour of flight, the pressure in her eardrums became so intense as they dropped that she instinctively cupped her bound hands over one of her ears while trying to shield the other with her shoulder. She felt the ship shudder. Then everything was still except for a dull vibration within the walls.

The drones grabbed her by both arms again and led her out of the ship. Grey sniffed and squared her shoulders, preparing herself for whatever came with as much strength as she could muster.

The cell where they dumped Grey reeked of sweat. The slab of a bed was stainless steel with scratches marring its surface, and the toilet and sink were steel too. A few strands of hair clumped over the drain in the floor.

She knew she was being watched as she carefully washed her wrists in the sink and tried not to wince at the sting of the water hitting the thin red lines the cuffs had dug into her skin. To calm her racing mind, she played back her visit with Mrs. March and hoped the officials here hadn't discovered a way to read thoughts. She'd heard of that.

Mrs. March had always been a little eccentric, but that's what Grey liked about her. She didn't fit any mold. But Jupiter? Had she really meant it when she said she'd flown convicts to the planet? It was hard to picture her as a Mazdaar pilot. Mrs. March was against everything they stood for.

A buzz came from the door, and two guards entered. Grey keyed herself up, glancing quickly into their fully-dilated pupils.

One had a scar on its forehead as if it had been injured. She didn't realize bioskin could repair like that.

"Turn around." The drone's voice had no fluctuation.

The restraints were clamped back on her wrists, a little looser than before.

They led her down a hallway, and her heart pumped in time with their footsteps. Passing through two security blocks where someone had to unlock the entrances for them, Grey quickly lost track of where she was. Even if she could fight these drones off, she wouldn't have a clue how to escape.

The drones stopped in front of an unmarked white door, pausing probably for whoever was inside to scan their brain chips for the information they'd gathered on Grey.

As soon as the door opened, the machines that looked like humans led her inside. It reminded her of when Carr had left them in that conference room waiting for Jet. Only instead of a luxurious, clear conference table, a black metal desk was placed squarely in the center. A leather chair was behind it with a molded plastic one in front.

The drones deposited Grey in the plastic chair, and she had to sit on its edge with her hands twisted behind her back. At least they'd let her keep her clothes, and she hadn't undergone a strip search since they'd performed a total body scan. Which meant they had to know she wasn't connected by now. Had they finally decided to crack down and force those on the outside to have the Mazdaar Communication Dot implanted?

Dot implants had first been introduced back when Mazdaar took power and the survivors of the War were in panic mode. No larger than a grain of rice and injected painlessly into a person's head or hand, they were given to everyone free of charge. All personal information could be stored in a Dot, and buying and selling was as easy as a hand swipe. People were eager to connect to the security and convenience Mazdaar offered.

Later, they upgraded to implants that could do more, including chips in the brain which operated by cognition. Combined with permanent ocelli lenses and auris plugs, they allowed a user to connect to all the networks, communicating easily with anyone, anywhere.

She almost hoped that was why she was here. If they forced her to get a Dot, they'd probably release her. There were procedures to remove them later, though they were painful.

Grey jumped as the wall beside her opened. When she saw the woman who entered, her pulse thumped.

General Evangeline Yurkutz glided into the room and stood behind the leather chair, her yellow eyes resting on Grey. A dark green cape flowed over one shoulder and down her back, the Mazdaar emblem prominently stitched to her sleeve. The general sat down at the desk, and dread surged through Grey. Mrs. March had warned her about this woman. Had they found out about her shooting the patroller?

The drones saluted, retreating back into the hallway and leaving Grey completely alone with someone she was sure wasn't above killing her just for sport.

"Since you are not connected, I will speak out loud for your benefit," General Yurkutz said in an accent Grey had never heard before.

"Where am I, and why am I here?" Grey scooted even farther toward the edge of her chair.

Yurkutz waved toward the wall behind her and a panel of floor-to-ceiling windows appeared. Grey cringed at the view. Glistening in the orange evening sun, a thousand sparkling buildings stretched toward the sky. If it wasn't utterly terrifying, it would've been breathtaking. This wasn't a painting on the wall of Jet's office. This was a window, and the long flight now made sense.

They'd taken her to Mazdaar City.

7

"W hy am I here?" Grey repeated.

She stood up to appear stronger than she felt. She was now on the other side of the world—as far from the Preserve as she could possibly be—and she had no idea why.

General Yurkutz folded her hands, and Grey noted the woman's fingernails were filed to points.

"I was surprised when your name came to my attention," Yurkutz said.

She knew her name?

"I wasn't aware my name would matter to someone like you." Grey kept her tone as respectful as possible.

The general stared at her with those weird eyes, and Grey almost wondered if she was fully human. Maybe they'd finally found a way to stabilize zoonotic genetics.

"You're Tanner and Sue Alexander's daughter."

She suddenly felt like a mouse in this lion's lair. "What do my parents have to do with this?"

"Everything." Leaning forward, the woman's eyes flicked up and to the right, and a life-size 3D hologram of Mom and Dad materialized beside them. It was all Grey could do to maintain her composure. They looked so real, just like the last time she'd seen them.

"I . . . I don't understand."

"Let me remind you that lying to me will get you nowhere."

Grey stared at the image of her parents. Seeing them again, even in this form, caused a rush of yearning.

"They're dead," Grey said softly.

"What did they tell you about their mission?"

The wire restraints seemed to pinch tighter, and Grey dropped down in the chair again. Mission? Dad fixed things, and Mom grew medicinal herbs. There was no mission other than to make sure she and Rin survived outside of Mazdaar long enough to grow up. She tore her eyes away from the image.

"I don't know about any mission."

"Really?" General Yurkutz raised an eyebrow.

Grey glanced at the hologram again. Frozen in place, her parents appeared to be staring at something in the distance. Both wore tan cargo pants and white tunics like they always had.

"I want to know what I'm charged with."

Yurkutz gave a slight laugh. Her hands were still folded. "Grey Alexander, you haven't been charged with anything, yet."

"Then why am I here?"

The Mazdaar general blinked twice, and the hologram disappeared. "Your charges will be dealt with in time, I assure you. On top of your smuggling activities, you have murdered a border patrol agent. Both merit strict punishment."

Grey's mouth suddenly felt as dry as her desert home. She had hoped the guard had survived. Taking a deep breath, she forced herself not to show any sign of guilt.

"And you are not connected. But you may be surprised to know that I do not really care about any of those things. I have different plans for you."

Grey balled her fingers into fists behind her back.

"Oh, you can try to be tough. But it won't be of much use, I'm afraid." Yurkutz leaned across the desk. "Mazdaar always wins. Your parents know this better than anyone. Now why don't we try this again. Where are they?"

What was she talking about? Grey had given up wishing Mom and Dad were still alive, and she didn't dare let herself hope again.

The general glared at her, and the smallest of smiles crept onto her lips. Suddenly, searing pain shot through the wire restraints into Grey's wrists and up her arms with the intensity of a lightning bolt. She braced against it. The pain arced down her spine radiating toward her legs, and a guttural cry came out of her mouth.

The pain left as quickly as it had come.

"Perhaps now you understand how important this is to me," General Yurkutz said.

Grey straightened, the back of her shirt now sticking to the plastic chair. She tried to catch her breath. "I . . . don't . . . know what you're talking about. And even if I did, I wouldn't tell you." Grey braced for another shock from the cuffs, but Yurkutz stood to her feet. She had to be at least six feet tall.

"I can see you will need some convincing," Yurkutz said.

The drones returned without warning and grabbed Grey by the arms again. She flinched at their touch. Their bioskin was warm. She tried to stand, but her legs almost gave out. Her muscles still trembling, the drones practically carried her out of the room. In one of the corridors, a group of men in black suits came toward them in the hallway. When Grey caught sight of the man in the long tailcoat, she called out.

"Jet?"

His eyes met hers, then darted away. Had he ratted on her?

The group parted for them as they passed, but Grey strained against her captors, twisting around to see Jet's form drift away.

"Jet! Jet, please!"

"Quiet," one of the drones said in a synthesized voice.

Jet kept walking and didn't look back.

Hiding in the alcove at the top of their silo, Rin had help-lessly watched them take Grey. It took everything in her to keep from racing out to try and rescue her sister. She'd held her hand over her mouth to keep from screaming. She knew why Grey hadn't run for home, and the tears hadn't stopped pouring from Rin's eyes since.

First Mom and Dad. Now her sister. How had they found Grey? They'd always made sure they weren't followed, taking every precaution possible. Grey wasn't stupid. She knew how to evade Mazdaar. They'd been doing it successfully for five years.

Huddled in the pine needles beside the zorses, Rin hadn't moved for hours. She was alone. Hunger nonexistent. Thirst nowhere to be found. The image of the catchship swallowing Grey up like an evil monster kept replaying in her mind.

She didn't know for sure how long she stayed in the pen, but when the entrance siren sounded, Rin frantically scrambled to her feet, brushing off the needles sticking to her canvas pants. Tram's and Trif's ears twitched toward the speaker in the ceiling above them.

For one moment, she thought it was Grey back with some wild story about how she'd escaped, and it hit her all over again that her sister was gone. She'd seen the insignia on the ship. Grey might never be back.

Rin dashed frantically through the door that led down to the living level. It automatically locked behind her. She closed herself into the silo's small control room and stared up at the security screens.

The entrance sensor only sounded if someone came within six feet of the door. Occasionally, a wild animal would set it off in the middle of the night, but Rin wasn't thinking animals now. Not after what happened to Grey.

Her forehead grew damp as she studied the video feed from the front entrance. A person—or was it a drone?—stood outside, face hidden from view by a dark hood. Rin mentally flipped through their emergency protocol. They had packs ready and waiting to grab. She might even have time to turn Tram and Trif loose in the escape tunnel.

Please. Not now. She couldn't do this without Grey.

Suddenly, the intruder turned toward the camera, retracting her hood. Her white hair and weathered face immediately came into view.

"It's me, Rin," Mrs. March said, looking up at the camera. "I'm alone, and no one followed me."

Rin quickly pressed her thumb onto the unlock sensor and rushed back up the stairs. When Mrs. March came down the ramp and met Rin at the second security door, Rin began to weep.

She could barely speak but managed to say, "They took Grey."

Wrapping her in a hug, Mrs. March patted her on the back as the door closed.

"I know. That's why I'm here, child."

"But how . . ." Rin gently broke the embrace, drying her tears with her sleeve. She only ended up smearing dirt across her cheeks.

"There's not a lot of time, but I'll explain what I can." Mrs. March led her toward the living level. "Is the cloaking shield still active?"

Rin nodded. Dad had invented a system years ago that hid their position from radar and heat sensors. Somehow he'd discovered how to duplicate the same frequency the surrounding rocks emitted, and once transmitted over the silo, any scanner would register their location as a pile of rocks.

As they passed the control room, Mrs. March gestured toward the screens. "May I?"

"I just checked them."

Studying the screens, her neighbor's hands flew across the controls. Rin watched in amazement as she maneuvered each camera to present a 360-degree view of their surroundings. Her eyes darting from screen to screen, Mrs. March pointed at the view up on the bluff, halting the camera's movement with a quick jab of a button.

"There."

"What?"

"See that speck in the sky?"

Rin squinted. "Maybe."

"They're already searching." Mrs. March kept her eyes on the screen. "That's an advanced Mazdaar military catchship like the one that took Grey. I was hoping we had more time."

Rin crossed her arms, bewildered. "What's going on?"

Mrs. March switched all the cameras back to their normal angles with familiarity and came to stand in front of her. She rested her hands on Rin's shoulders. "We have a lot to talk about."

⊹

Back in her cell, Grey closed her eyes and the vivid hologram of her parents sprang to her mind. She and Rin had only one photographic image of them. Taken on their wedding day, she'd always wished for something more recent to jog her memory as to how they'd looked when she was growing up. The hologram General Yurkutz showed her was exactly what Mom and Dad looked like the day they didn't come home. Did she dare hope they could still be alive?

She shook her head and examined her wrists. The shock cuffs had left deeper, angrier lines than before. As frightened as she was, Grey was relieved that it was her in this cell and not Rin. She would never have been able to forgive herself if her little sister had been taken. She only hoped Rin would have the strength to go on if she didn't get back.

And the more Grey thought about it, the more she realized that was probably what would happen. They wouldn't take a prisoner all the way to Mazdaar City if they intended to release them anytime soon.

When her cell door finally opened, Grey jumped up. Expecting a stoic drone, she was shocked when Jet stepped into the cell.

"Please, help me, Jet," she pleaded.

"I will do everything I can." The door shut behind him.

"Why am I here? What are they—"

He held up his hand. "Grey, we have exactly thirty seconds before my block on their devices expires. I have little time to explain, but know this—I did not betray you." He pointed at her wrists. "Be brave, and please trust me."

She nodded, trying not to cry. She didn't dare utter Rin's

name, but she wanted to beg him to look after her sister and Mrs. March.

"I haven't been forthright, but that was to protect you." Jet stared straight into her eyes and held her hand in both of his. Only a few inches taller than she, somehow she felt he could take down a man twice his size. It was rumored he had advanced belts in just about every kind of martial arts.

"You didn't turn me in?"

"I did not."

"They think my parents are alive. Could they be?"

Jet blinked and glanced upward, and she knew her chance for any answer was gone.

"They will hold a council later today. Your punishment will be decided there."

All Grey could do was nod and watch Jet turn and leave the cell, his coat flapping behind him.

"Your parents weren't able to tell you many things," Mrs. March said.

They sat at the triangular table Rin and Grey had eaten breakfast on only this morning. Rin took a deep breath and studied their friend who seemed to be full of surprises.

"Do you know where they took Grey?"

"My suspicion is Mazdaar City, but we will know for sure soon."

Rin's heart sunk. Mazdaar City was known for its harsh treatment of prisoners. She rested her head on her arms, overcome by what this meant for her sister.

"Listen to me." Mrs. March reached across the table and stroked her hair.

Rin lifted her head. "What are they doing to her?"

"As long as they think she has information, she'll be okay."

"Information about what?"

Mrs. March sighed. "What do you know about Jupiter, child?"

Oh, great. Now Mrs. March really was sounding crazy.

"It's the key to all of this."

"Jupiter?"

"I told Grey a few things when she visited today, but not everything. I'd intended to explain everything to you both."

"I don't know anything about Jupiter."

"I thought not. Your parents didn't want to involve either of you until you were older."

She eyed the old woman. "What are you talking about?"

Rising from her chair, Mrs. March looked down at her with concern. "Jupiter is habitable; that's the first thing you should know."

"But the atmosphere is—"

"Unbreathable." Mrs. March gestured in the air. "I know. That's exactly what Mazdaar wants you to believe. But they've changed that now. It's all over the zones that Jupiter *is* habitable. Right now, Rin, it's important you understand that beneath the swirling clouds and Jupiter winds, a world more majestic than this one exists. In the right hands, this discovery would've been the greatest our world has ever known. In the wrong hands, it's devastating to our entire race, and that's what we're looking at right now."

Rin stared at the plastic tabletop, wondering if she'd made a mistake in letting Mrs. March inside. Yet the spark in Mrs. March's eyes and the earnestness of her voice didn't seem like that of a demented old lady. And if it hadn't been for Mrs. March these past few years, she wasn't sure they would've survived.

"What does this have to do with Grey?"

Mrs. March crouched down beside her, knees creaking.

"Believe me when I say we don't have much time." Mrs. March went to the door leading down to the silo's lower levels. She pressed her thumb to the reader, and it opened for her.

Rin's mouth gaped. "How did—"

"There are things you don't know about me too," Mrs. March said.

They kept Grey in restraints while she waited outside the Council chamber, flanked again by two drones. These wore crisp, military dress whites with green sashes and belts. Fear swirled in her, and Jet's appearance in her cell had only confused her more. Was he really a friend?

She stared at the huge, wooden double doors of the chamber. Snakes and gargoyles were carved into the wood, all writhing around the Mazdaar star with the triple spiral at its center. Large and ornate, looking totally out of place in this otherwise sterile facility, they seemed to broadcast the importance of the room beyond.

General Yurkutz would be in there.

When the doors finally parted, they swung outward in the ancient style rather than sliding sideways into a pocket in the wall. Two men ushered her and the guards inside.

Grey's eyes were immediately drawn to the glass ceiling thirty feet above them. She stared up at the puffy clouds floating smoothly across a dark blue expanse. She'd do just about anything to be enjoying that view with Rin up on the ridge right now.

The drone on her right shoved her toward a row of benches in the middle of the room. These faced a platform where seven sleek, white ergonomic chairs waited for their occupants.

Several other people in restraints were already seated on the benches. A bald man with a scar running down his cheek peered her way. She was the only girl in the room.

The drones ordered her to sit. She did, staring down at her wrists. At least they'd bound her hands in front this time, but the cords still pinched mercilessly.

The High Council strode in from the opposite side of the room. Grey had read that each member had been chosen personally by the Chancellor and represented each of the seven sectors of Mazdaar society: military, agriculture, banking, police, religion, medicine, and politics. Evangeline Yurkutz represented the military branch.

Grey had only ever seen holograms of the four men and three women who made up the High Council, including Yurkutz. They had authority to change law and condemn the guilty and innocent alike, and they looked even more imposing here in the flesh. Their burgundy robes flowed like flags as they walked. All of them appeared frozen at the age of forty.

Grey didn't see Jet anywhere.

"Let it be stated Council is now in session," a booming voice announced from invisible speakers that made it sound like the words came from every direction.

A Councilman with a scrawny goatee who was sitting next to General Yurkutz cleared his throat, glaring down at the prisoners. His eyes were the color of his robe, a deep, unnatural maroon.

"We will begin with the case of Matthew Salinas. Please rise, Mr. Salinas."

The prisoner with the bald head stood. His hands were bound with thicker wire than hers. He started to speak. "Please, your Honor, I would like to—"

Before the man could finish his sentence, his face contorted in pain. He gritted his teeth and let out a growl that sounded like the badger Grey had disturbed on her walk home last week. She realized he was being shocked.

"You will speak only when asked, Mr. Salinas."

The man nodded, his face shiny with sweat. Several of the other prisoners murmured to each other but were quickly silenced by their drone guards.

"We have reviewed your case in depth, so we will not waste anyone's time with meaningless rhetoric. We will ask you one question, Mr. Salinas."

The current was still coursing through the prisoner's body. Grey couldn't watch the man struggle against the pain. She turned away. General Yurkutz was actually smiling as she watched the man suffer.

Only when the man sunk to his chair doubled over did the shock release. Were they making him an example to the rest of the prisoners?

Grey carefully watched a Council member with long, blonde hair seated at the center of the table. Her eyes kept darting back and forth without focusing, the typical nystagmus of the connected. What kind of mind-to-mind communication was happening between these people? Were the briefs and evidence sheets stored in their Dots, ready to be called up to their minds?

"Did you," the blonde woman finally asked, "or did you not participate in the protest at the Chancellor's coronation?"

Slowly standing to his feet again, Mr. Salinas squared his shoulders. His jaw muscle twitched.

"Lady Kern asked you a question," General Yurkutz said.

"Speak," the Council member with the goatee demanded.

Mr. Salinas swayed for a moment then caught himself. "I would do it again."

Inwardly, Grey winced for the man.

"That is all we need to know," Lady Kern said, and each Council member nodded.

Staring straight ahead, Yurkutz seemed to be reading something within her cranial field of vision. Grey was having trouble following these strange procedures. Where were the advocates for the prisoners? Had their arguments already been presented?

"Our ruling is unanimously guilty." The general scowled down at the prisoner. "Punishment is death, to be executed publicly tomorrow."

A gasp came from a prisoner sitting behind Grey. She could only watch Mr. Salinas be half carried, half dragged out of the room.

"The case of Grey Alexander is called." Lady Kern's authoritative voice made Grey's legs instantly weak.

"Please rise, Miss Alexander."

Rin usually avoided Dad's workshop. The few times she'd been down here in the past five years had made her cry, remembering how much he loved spending time fiddling with his tools and gadgets.

Grey was the one who snuck in here on a regular basis. She'd usually come down when she thought Rin was sleeping, like she had the other night. Rin wondered if it helped Grey hang on to the hope that their parents might still be alive.

"I would imagine your father didn't tell you much about his work," Mrs. March said.

She went from surface to surface in the workshop, surveying what Tanner Alexander had left behind.

"I never asked him," Rin said. "Grey's the curious one."

Mrs. March smiled. "I've always loved that about her. And your tender heart is what makes you special, Rin."

"You said we don't have much time?" Rin held her arms around her body as if warding off a cold wind. "I'm not a child. I want to know what's going on."

Mrs. March came closer and stared down at her. Her take-charge presence was reassuring.

"If they took Grey to Mazdaar City, how can we possibly help her?" Rin asked.

"I have people there already watching for her. In fact . . ." Mrs. March pulled a copper medallion necklace out from under her tunic. The disconnected had to rely on external controllers to do a fraction of what the Dots did for the connected. Mrs. March pressed the medallion, and a tiny holographic image appeared in front of her.

Rin's mouth gaped when she saw it was Jet.

"What is he—"

Mrs. March shushed her. "Just give me a minute." She studied the image. "Any news?"

"They took her to the High Council," Jet said.

"Then it's as we suspected."

"Her case is being called now. Have you activated *Tevah?*"

"Working on it."

"Must go."

Jet's image disappeared.

Mrs. March rushed over to the wall with the hidden panel that led to the one room in the silo Rin had only visited twice. Her thumbprint caused the panel to slide open for them, and Rin didn't bother asking anymore how Mrs. March had access to the home that was supposed to be coded only for her family.

"Jet will do what he can for Grey, but in the meantime, you and I have work to do."

Rin had to jog to keep up with the old woman. "But how can Jet possibly help Grey?"

Mrs. March didn't answer. Catching up, Rin grabbed Mrs. March by the shirtsleeve in the darkness of the corridor. Lit only by the dim solar lamps, the hair sticking out from her head gave her a mad-scientist look.

Mrs. March glanced down at Rin's hand on her sleeve, but Rin didn't release her. "This is my home, and she's my sister. I need to know what's going on."

The woman's face softened. "I'd forgotten how determined an Alexander can be. You're right. You do deserve answers, Rin. I don't have all of them, but I will give you what I have. But can we continue moving?"

She let Mrs. March go, and their footsteps echoed off the corridor walls as they hurried. Rin stepped over a puddle that had formed in the corner.

"Years ago, I contracted your parents," Mrs. March said.

"You did? For what?"

"To develop Operation Noah in this region."

Rin rubbed her eyes. "I have no idea what that means."

"And you shouldn't. They had to keep it completely confidential." Mrs. March cued the final door to open, and Rin followed her out onto the catwalk of the room where the missiles used to be housed. "You knew about the cosmoship *Tevah* though, right?"

Rin swallowed and stared at the huge spacecraft that had sat dormant for as long as she could remember. "Dad showed me, but I never knew its name."

Frowning, Mrs. March keyed the lights on, melting the shadows. "I had a feeling. He shouldn't have, but your father was a wise man. I'm sure he had his reasons."

With both hands on the railing, she looked energized by seeing the ship, and her features flushed. Rin took in her ramrod spine, the confident way she spoke. She thought about everything she'd ever known about this woman.

"Mrs. March, who are you?"

Turning around, the old woman put her hands on her hips. Water dripped somewhere, and a faint hum came from one of the lights.

Mrs. March took in a deep breath. "I am Commander Fleur March of the Yien Dynasty's Special Forces."

10

Grey arose from her chair, legs wobbly. She'd just seen a man condemned to death, but she would not cower. No matter how afraid she might be. She systematically met eyes with each Council member, first General Yurkutz, then the others.

"How old are you?"

The question came from the Councilman on the far left. He wore a chunky ring on each of his fingers. She thought he represented the banking sector. Didn't they already have all her personal information?

"Speak," Yurkutz ordered.

"Seventeen," Grey said.

"Why are you here?"

She swallowed hard. Was this a trick question?

"I . . . I'm . . ."

"You do have a tongue, correct?" This came from Lady Kern.

Grey exhaled. "I don't know why I'm here."

The Council members exchanged looks. She saw Yurkutz roll her eyes.

"I find that very hard to believe," the man with the rings said.

"You seem to think I know something about my parents," Grey said.

"Go on."

"But I don't!" She braced for a shock, but it didn't come. "As far as I know, they died five years ago."

Lady Kern stared at her with orbs as cold as moons. "What crimes have you committed, Miss Alexander?"

Grey looked down. Great. What hole had she dug for herself? Could they pry a confession out of her against her will?

Somehow she felt she had to stand up to these people. "If you don't already know, you aren't as powerful as I was led to believe."

The jolt that suddenly shot through her wrists emanated up her arms and into her chest. It took hold of her muscles and shook them, burning through her head and making it feel like it would explode.

Grey's determination to be bold melted onto the floor as a cry she barely recognized as her own escaped from her lips. She tried to lift her head and see if the Council was enjoying watching her suffer like they had with Salinas, but she couldn't. She dropped to her knees, curling into herself.

"Stop!" A voice came from beside her.

But the pain did not stop, and Grey felt herself drifting into unconsciousness.

A strong hand grabbed her cuffs, and she heard something snap. Instantly the shock ceased, and Grey was lifted to her feet and set back into her chair.

"Stay with me. Breathe."

She couldn't see.

"Grey, look at me."

Gasping, she focused on the blurry man kneeling in front of her.

Jet.

He sprang to his feet, fists balled. Dangling from one of his gloved hands were her restraints. Jet threw them to the floor in front of the Council. "You make a mockery of justice!"

"And you of the Crown." Lady Kern's voice dripped with disgust.

Grey half expected the drones to rush him and drag him away, but they looked on, stoic as ever. She wondered if he'd remotely altered their programs. The other prisoners stared at Jet in horror as if they expected a bolt of lightning to strike him dead on the spot.

"I will not stand by and watch you torture a girl who has done nothing to warrant this kind of treatment."

Evangeline Yurkutz leveled her gaze on Jet. "You are a man of conflicted loyalties."

Grey struggled to move her limbs. Slowly, her senses returned. The pain was gone, but its effect on her muscles left her drained, as if she hadn't slept for days. She watched Jet's back. He was wearing a uniform she'd never seen before. It was black with white stripes down the sleeves, across his chest, and down the sides of his pants. On each shoulder a gold, circular emblem that looked like a rising sun almost glowed. How much authority did he have here? They were letting him address them as equals.

"I expected this Council to seek the truth and issue justice accordingly."

"You are interfering with this justice you speak of," the man from the banking district said.

Jet pointed at Grey. "This Council was instituted to ferret

out criminals who threatened our great Unified World. Now you silence the voices of conscientious objectors. I do not call that justice."

"This girl is not innocent," Yurkutz said. "And I am already questioning her usefulness. I had hoped she would lead us to greater things."

"If you're talking about my parents," Grey said, her scratchy throat causing her voice to crack. Without the fear of a shock, she could at least say one more thing. "You're right. I would never betray them. No matter what you do to me."

Jet glanced at her, and she thought she saw the corners of his mouth turn up.

"Quiet!" Lady Kern said. "You are a criminal. You have smuggled illegal items, resisted connection, and murdered a border patroller. All of these actions are punishable by law."

"They should be dealt with in a local jurisdiction," Jet said. "She does not need to be here in front of you."

"Yet here she is," Yurkutz said.

Grey's head was starting to ache. For a moment, the edges of her vision darkened again.

"I present a proposition," Jet said.

Lady Kern rolled her eyes. "Pray, tell. I can only imagine what."

"Release her into my custody as a token of goodwill between Mazdaar and the Yien Dynasty. We will see to her trial and proper punishment."

The panel was still. She saw something flick in the Mazdaar general's feline eyes. Grey's fate was in Jet's hands now, and she still didn't know for sure if she could trust him. The Yien Dynasty? What was he talking about?

Each Council member's eyes began to twitch, and Grey wished she was privy to their telepathic communication.

"Remove the other prisoners," General Yurkutz finally

ordered, and immediately the drones herded their charges out the door. Grey turned to watch. They were as helpless as she was, but she still wished they wouldn't leave her. The room was cleared, and silence spread throughout the cavernous space.

Yurkutz fixed an icy look on Jet. "You are treading on shaky ground, Mr. Yien."

"But you will acknowledge the merit of my suggestion." Jet didn't wait for them to respond. "As you know, Grey Alexander is no ordinary girl."

It was the first time she'd heard his surname. Who was Jet, after all?

"Silence!" Yurkutz slammed her fist on the table, quaking the water in the crystal goblets placed in front of each Council member.

Jet seemed to be in deep thought. The communication Dots worked by the user thinking a command, usually a series of connected words not normally thought in everyday life. Advanced users could implement several tasks at once, and she guessed Jet was patching into the Council's frequency. She didn't understand the sudden secrecy. What would they need to discuss that she couldn't hear?

Time ceased as Grey tried to make sense of their facial expressions. Each of them stared straight ahead, silently arguing about her. She ran her fingers through her hair, now damp with sweat. Her life was at stake, and she had no idea what Jet was saying on her behalf.

She thought of Rin again and once more was glad it was she in this strange place facing these merciless people rather than her tenderhearted sister.

The man with the rings was the first to speak. "Then it is decided."

What was decided?

Jet gave a slight bow. "You have chosen wisely."

He turned to Grey and motioned for her to rise. When she tried to stand her knees buckled, but Jet grabbed hold of her with a strong grip and helped her to her feet. He firmly led her from the room even as the Council scowled at them with looks that could kill.

11

Outside the chamber, Jet relaxed his hold on Grey's arm and ignored the curious looks from the other prisoners waiting in the corridor. Even the drones eyed him with almost intelligent awe. Grey knew better than to speak. She didn't understand what had just happened anymore than she understood why she was here in Mazdaar City, but somehow she wanted to believe she was safer with Jet than at the mercy of the Council.

"Where are we going?" she whispered when they were out of ear shot.

"You'll return to your cell for now," Jet said.

She nodded, understanding he couldn't say more where they were. "How did you get them to release me?"

He smiled, small wrinkles appearing around his eyes. Maybe he hadn't had age-enhancement surgery after all.

"My father is Emperor Yien."

Grey felt her own eyes widen.

"It does have its advantages." Jet smiled again. "From which you have now benefited."

They continued down the corridor, and Grey noticed that each official or drone they passed gave Jet a wide berth. How much influence did this man really have?

Jet leaned toward her ear. "It would be best if you appeared frightened of me."

She wondered if she actually might be. Yes, he'd saved her from the Mazdaar Council, but how could she have done business with him all these years and not known he was the emperor's son?

When they reached the open cell, Jet pushed her inside and left without another word. Grey sunk down onto the metal bunk. Her limbs still felt weak, and a persistent buzz seemed to be vibrating her eardrums.

She lifted her arms and examined her wrists. The restraints had burned deeper into her flesh, causing purple blood to push to the surface. Grey closed her eyes. Not knowing what tomorrow would bring was something she and Rin had gotten used to, but this kind of uncertainty was hard to take. At least back home she was the one choosing to put herself at risk when she'd traded or sold contraband. Here, she was at the mercy of powers she didn't even understand. And she was still a prisoner.

Rin watched Mrs. March deftly work the controls as panels on the massive silo wall opened and closed. Long metal arms extended toward the blue cosmoship. She'd spent the last several minutes peppering her neighbor with questions. Some Mrs. March had answered; others she brushed off for another time.

"Do you have any idea how weird all this sounds?"

Mrs. March laughed. "I can imagine."

"I still don't understand what you're doing here."

"Now you know in part; then you shall know fully."

"What?"

Mrs. March searched Rin's face. "Don't you remember your parents reciting the Scriptures to you?"

Barely.

Turning toward her, Mrs. March's face softened. "Rin, I know this is hard. Please understand I am very aware of what's at stake here for you. I will do everything in my power to keep your family intact. We are working—" the woman pulled out her medallion controller.

Rin caught sight of Jet's image again.

"I have news," he said.

"Proceed," Mrs. March responded.

"They have surrendered her to my custody."

Mrs. March's shoulders relaxed. She smiled at Rin. "Wonderful. You'll escort her?"

"Yes."

"Good job."

"My pleasure, Commander." Rin didn't think she'd ever get used to Mrs. March being called Commander.

They signed off, and Rin was about to barrage Mrs. March again when the woman began to explain.

"Grey's okay," she said. "Jet's making sure of it."

Mrs. March slipped the necklace back under her tunic. "Jet's not exactly who you might have thought. For quite some time now you've been smuggling contraband, correct?"

"Just like you taught us to do." Rin fiddled with the frayed edge of her sleeve cuff. "Grey wouldn't let me come at first, but she has for the past year."

"I'm glad she's looked out for you."

Rin tipped her chin up, trying to keep from crying.

Everything was going to be all right. Grey was coming home. "She's the best sister ever."

Mrs. March grinned. "How much do you know about the Yien Dynasty?"

She shrugged.

"Mazdaar might act like they own the world, but they do not. Not all of it." Mrs. March flipped a switch, and more lights came on around the silo. "Most of Asia is still ruled by the Yiens, and it's their goal to spread the truth about Mazdaar's lies into every zone. But they must do it secretly. You and Grey have actually been involved in Yien initiatives for quite some time now."

"We have?"

"As your parents were before you. You've been carrying messages from the outside to Yien operatives like me without even knowing it. It was the only way I knew to help provide for you. I made sure they paid you well."

"But Jet's shorted us more than once."

"That was planned." Mrs. March gave a small nod. "It was his way to signal to me if Mazdaar was close to discovering you rather than contacting me directly, which is always risky. Jet has dual citizenship, and his access to Mazdaar has given us much intelligence. He probably saved your sister's life today."

"So everything's going to be okay?"

Mrs. March sighed. "I hope so. But unfortunately, we're not out of danger yet."

12

Grey was barely able to eat the bland mash shoved through the slot in her cell door that afternoon. A disgusting mixture that tasted like rotten corn, she forced it down to keep up her strength but soon regretted it. Her stomach now churned.

She lay on the bed, closing her burning eyes. She could still remember how safe and warm she'd felt when her father would hug her all those years ago and the way Mom seemed to know what she was thinking without a word spoken. Could it really be true? Were they still alive?

The cell door slid open, and Grey shot to her feet. The food had helped one thing, anyway. Her headache had faded with the nourishment.

None other than General Evangeline Yurkutz marched into the cell, and Grey instinctively shrunk back from her.

"Expecting your savior?" Yurkutz laughed. "Did you think we would allow him to take you away so easily?"

Grey's shoulders drooped. "What do you want with me?"

"I think we've already established that." Yurkutz signaled a drone that entered the small space as well. "Restrain her."

Grey tensed, ready to fight.

"If you resist, you will regret it," the general said.

"Why don't I doubt that?"

The drone jerked her arms behind her back and tied them securely with new restraints made of thicker wire than before. She wondered if their shock would be stronger.

Grey had to look up to meet Evangeline Yurkutz's eyes, but she did so just to show her defiance. She would not appear weak in front of this woman.

Yurkutz slapped her across the face, and Grey almost fell from the strength of her hand.

Without thinking, she launched herself at the woman, barreling her shoulder into the general's chest. Air whooshed from Yurkutz's lungs, but just as quickly, she threw Grey to the floor in some martial arts maneuver she didn't see coming. With her hands bound behind her back and unable to break her fall, Grey's head made contact with the cement, and everything went black.

When she came to, she found herself strapped into the seat of a two-person vehicle zooming down what looked like the main thoroughfare of Mazdaar City. Dozens of similar cars silently glided alongside them, all piloting themselves and guided by satellite and sensors embedded in the polymeric pavement. Grey had heard about them but had never seen them before.

Her arms were still tied behind her back, and her shoulders ached from the strain. How long had she been unconscious?

"That was a stupid move," Yurkutz said, and Grey jumped when she realized who sat beside her.

"Yet so satisfying," Grey muttered, expecting to be shocked. When she was not, she wondered if the general was saving that pleasure for later.

"Apparently, your parents passed their stubborn genes to their offspring."

"If this is still about them, you're wasting your time."

"I don't waste anything."

"How many times do I have to say I don't know where they are?" Grey shifted in her seat. "I thought they were dead."

"So did we."

A spark flickered in Grey's heart. Yurkutz wasn't denying they were alive any more than Jet was. But if they weren't dead, why hadn't they come home?

"Why do you even care about them?" Grey stared out the blue-tinted window. If her hands had been free, she might've tried to jump out into the street, even if they were probably traveling over one hundred kilometers per hour.

General Yurkutz tapped Grey's leg with her index finger, and she recoiled at the woman's touch. She wore a ring with a huge ruby embedded into the silver-like metal, probably platinum.

"You Alexanders are so unusual. You stick together. Family means something to you. Rather old fashioned, but in this case it's going to be helpful."

"I don't know where they are!" Grey swung around to face her. "Do you want me to make something up? You can torture me all you want, but the answer's still the same."

"Did I say I didn't know where they are?"

Grey struggled to keep her emotions from her face.

Yurkutz studied her for a moment, then laughed. "You really did think they were dead, didn't you?"

She would not answer this woman. Would not. But inside, Grey was screaming. They were alive. Alive!

"What I actually asked you earlier was where are they *hiding?*" The general leaned closer, her spicy perfume almost causing Grey to sneeze. "There's a difference."

Grey turned toward the window again as they blew through an intersection. Even though the air inside the car was warm, a chill spread through her body. She focused on the pain in her sore muscles and tried not to think about what methods a woman like Evangeline Yurkutz could use to pry things out of her. At least for a prisoner with information, relief would come if they shared their secrets.

The general tapped Grey's leg again, like she knew how much it creeped her out. "But even birds can be flushed out if necessary," she said.

Mrs. March had been examining *Tevah*'s exterior for the past hour. She'd climbed the scaffolding Rin had never even noticed along the silo's walls, using a strange eyepiece that allowed her to zoom in on every crack and crevice as if she was directly on top of it. She was checking the ship's surface for any faults without even touching it.

"Looking good, darling," Mrs. March cooed affectionately to the ship as if it could hear her, and more than once Rin mistakenly thought she was speaking to her.

"Does this thing actually fly?" Rin called up to where she'd last seen the old woman.

"I hope so."

When Mrs. March finally finished her inspection, a satisfied smile spread across her face. She dropped down from the scaffolding in front of Rin, and Rin shook her head at how lithe the eighty-plus-year-old was.

"Why is this thing even in our silo?"

"I'm surprised you didn't ask me sooner."

"When I would ask Dad, he'd tell me to forget I'd even seen it. Kinda hard to do, you know?"

Mrs. March chuckled. "Tanner should never have allowed you down here."

"You're letting me," Rin said.

"I wasn't given much choice."

"Please answer my question."

Pulling a rag from her pocket, Mrs. March wiped her soiled fingers. "Did you ever wonder what your father was working on late at night in his shop back here?"

"He loved to tinker with things."

Mrs. March stared up at the ship, and Rin watched in awe as the outline of a huge opening appeared in the hull.

Mrs. March waved toward it. "Care to join me for a tour? I'll explain as we go."

"Where are you taking me?"

The car seemed to speed even faster through tunnels, over bridges, well beyond the city limits. They'd twisted and turned through the streets until the road widened. Years ago, vehicles like these were actually driven by their occupants. People were always crashing into each other. Now, the vehicles moved in concert, traveling as close as three inches apart but never colliding.

Evangeline Yurkutz stared straight ahead, her eyes twitching. Grey shut up. The general could've had any drone transport her, and yet she was personally escorting Grey.

"Why do you care so much about my parents?"

Yurkutz blinked but gave no other indication she'd heard Grey.

"I deserve to know."

"You deserve nothing."

"What have they done?"

A sneer came to her lips, but she said nothing more. Grey knew she was toying with her life by pressing the issue. She looked out the window again. A desert even more vast than hers at home shot past, and she longed to be curling up in one of their plush chairs watching a movie with Rin like they had the other night. She felt light years away from home. Was her sister okay, or had they captured her too?

Oh, God, please keep Rin safe.

The traffic thinned, and Grey tried to guess where they were going. She knew little about the geography surrounding Mazdaar City, but when she spotted long, concrete airstrips, she guessed this was their destination. Maneuvering onto a secondary road, the car slowed to approach a guardhouse. An armed human—she could clearly see his eyes—walked up to Yurkutz's side of the car. Her window opened, seemingly on its own.

"Good evening, General." The man saluted, and the chain-link gate opened. Grey tried to take in as much detail as she could in case the opportunity to escape presented itself. The fence would probably be electrified like the one at the border— impossible to dig under with just her hands.

The vehicle slid through, and dread gripped Grey as she watched the gate close behind them.

"There is no escape," Yurkutz said.

Grey was starting to believe her.

13

Rin stared up the metal ramp that led into the cosmoship. Mrs. March beckoned her to follow, but she hesitated. How could Dad have been working on this giant vessel for so long without talking about it?

Mrs. March looked over her shoulder. "I need to inspect the interior, dear."

Rin finally followed, boots clanking on the huge ramp and echoing through the silo. Sensory lights flicked on at their approach, and Rin found herself entering the bottom hold of the ship. She blinked at the sight. Strapped down and poised as if waiting for them were two Jeeps that looked like they were made in 2012. So old they might even run on petroleum.

"How long has this stuff been in here?" Rin turned around in a circle, taking in the crates of equipment. There were even several stalls that seemed ready to hold animals.

"Since before you were born," Mrs. March said, and for the first time, Rin felt like maybe she could actually call her

Commander. The woman stood erect with her head high, as if she was used to giving orders. Rin had always thought of her as an eccentric, elderly, and maybe even frail neighbor. She was anything but.

Mrs. March gestured toward a set of spiral stairs. "How much do you remember of the Scriptures, Rin?"

"Only a little." Her sister had just about given up on God even being real after Mom and Dad had disappeared. Grey figured if He hadn't been able to keep their family together there wasn't much point in trusting Him with anything else.

But Rin wasn't so sure. Sometimes she still whispered prayers.

"Noah was a man who lived thousands of years ago. God called him to build a great ship to rescue as many people as he could from a worldwide flood. He obeyed, and we're all descended from him." Mrs. March glanced back at her. "The Yien Dynasty built this cosmoship to rescue people too. Not from a flood of water, but a flood of evil. Mazdaar is determined to wipe us off the face of the earth, and it's our mission to survive."

Mrs. March swiped her palm over a scanner by an entryway, and it opened for her. Rin caught a glimpse of a room full of bunks.

"But how?"

Mrs. March crossed the floor. "This isn't the only ship we've built. There are hundreds more, all strategically placed in various parts of the world. There's even another one in the northern part of the Preserve." Mrs. March paused. "Do you know who Jet really is?"

Rin shook her head.

"He is Emperor Yien's son and heir."

"You're kidding."

"Mazdaar grows stronger every day. So far, they have not

directly challenged the Yien Dynasty. If Mazdaar tries to overthrow them, which they probably will soon, we must have somewhere to evacuate our people. That's why we cannot afford for Mazdaar to claim Jupiter like they have conquered most of Earth. And Mars."

Her words made sense, but all Rin really cared about was her sister. "Why did they have to take Grey? Was it because of the patroller she shot? That was my fault, Mrs. March. She was protecting me."

"It might have nothing to do with that. We think they took her because they are desperate to find your parents."

"But . . . they're dead."

Saying out loud the fact she'd tried so hard to deny caused a weight to press down on Rin. She'd hoped beyond hope for years, but Grey was probably right. She'd been naive to keep it up all these years. They weren't coming back.

Mrs. March rested her hand on Rin's shoulder. "Remember when I told you there was a lot you didn't know?"

She nodded. That was an understatement.

Mrs. March hesitated, glancing upward for a moment. She seemed to be weighing her words.

"What is it?"

The old woman squeezed her shoulder. "We think your parents may be alive."

Rin blinked. Then blinked again. "*What?*"

"I've wanted to tell you, but I wasn't sure."

"Are you serious? They're alive?"

"We think so, but I don't want to give you false hope, Rin. We don't know for sure."

Rin suddenly felt like she was five years old in a summer rainstorm, wanting to dance at the sheer joy of feeling cool water droplets hitting her flushed cheeks.

"I can't believe it!" Rin threw her arms around Mrs.

March, spinning them both around in a circle. "I mean I want to, but . . . I can't!"

Mrs. March laughed. "The fact that they took Grey might confirm Mazdaar believes it as well."

Rin tried to concentrate on Mrs. March's words, but her mind was whirring in a million directions. What would they look like now? Would they be proud of her?

"What happened to them? Where did they go?"

"They weren't on a hunting trip."

"Where do you think they are? Why haven't they come back?"

Mrs. March leaned close, cupping Rin's chin with her hand. "I may have said too much already, but you needed to know that much. Without Tanner and Sue, Operation Noah wouldn't exist here. They joined us to save lives. Your dad is the reason this ship is even here, and your mom . . . well, she would've been the one to fly it."

Rin pictured her mother kneeling in the dirt, carefully watering her herbs up on the bluff. "Mom?"

"Captain Alexander was . . . *is* the best pilot we have."

"This is just . . ." Rin let out a sharp exhale. "Wow."

With a wave, Mrs. March escorted Rin into the sleeping quarters. It seemed like over a hundred beds were crammed inside, some stacked four high.

"But if Mom's not here, who's going to fly it?"

Commander March grinned. "The second best pilot we have."

"And that would be?" she asked, already guessing the answer.

Climbing the circular staircase in the center of the ship, she was almost at the top before Rin could catch up with her.

"That would be me," Mrs. March said.

❖

Massive jets and cosmoships silently passed overhead, and Grey could feel her pulse throbbing against the wrist restraints. They maneuvered through a second guard post even more imposing than the first with razor wire topping the fence. For a second she thought this guard was human too, but then she saw its metal-claw hands. The drone wore the typical green fatigues of the Mazdaar MPs, and its gun was casually slung across its back. She recognized the muzzle as a blueflare laser. Not as powerful as the greens, which could kill instantly, but definitely more potent than the violet handhelds. She'd never survive a direct hit.

By the time the vehicle pulled up to a hangar that could've housed every single person Grey knew in the Preserve, panic took over. Briefly, her hopes had glimmered when Jet rescued her from the Council chamber, but they were long gone, replaced with the dread of what General Yurkutz had in store for her. Did Jet know she was gone? Would he rescue her again? Had they killed him?

As the statuesque woman got out, Grey contemplated making a run for it. But they were completely surrounded by guards. Whether they were human or drone Grey couldn't tell, because their eyes were covered with silver, opaque goggles, and they all wore gloves with no skin visible. One guard dragged Grey from the car, and the rest fell into step around her and Yurkutz as she was marched across the black pavement toward the hanger.

They passed through the manual door, which was opened from inside, and a dark-skinned, muscular man met them. He clicked his heels and saluted.

"General Yurkutz."

"When is liftoff?" Yurkutz asked.

"We are on schedule, General."

Evangeline Yurkutz gave a slight nod of her head. That's when the man turned to look at Grey. His eyes narrowed.

"Will she cause trouble?"

"She knows what will happen if she does."

"Good. Because I have the other passengers to think about."

He saluted again, then turned on his heels and walked across the hangar. A forklift zoomed past, loaded with cargo in metal crates marked with stenciled white numbers, and the Mazdaar general prodded Grey to walk. She stumbled forward. The restraints dug into her flesh, but she didn't dare ask her to loosen them.

The drone deposited Grey in a cell along the perimeter of the hangar and finally removed her restraints before slamming the door on her. It was nothing more than a five-by-five cage with a small, barred hole high in the door. If she stood on her toes, she could just see out into the huge building.

Grey ran her fingers through her dirty hair. She'd do anything to be back home with Rin right now, but Grey also knew if she kept thinking about her little sister her resolve would melt. It was better to focus on the here and now. And escape if possible.

Leaning against the wall, Grey slid down and crumpled to the floor. This was about her parents. They'd made that very clear. But why did Mazdaar even *care* about Tanner and Sue Alexander? Sure, they had been outlaws, but hardly worth pursuing like this. Did they know something about the regime?

She thought about the cosmoship in the missile silo. Was that what they were after? She would never tell them about that. It would lead them straight to Rin, something Grey would rather die than do. With a sigh, she climbed back to her feet and peered out into the hangar.

Grey watched the crews bustle about with supplies, loading them into various vessels. Occasionally, she'd spot an armed guard watching from the sidelines, but most of the personnel seemed to be civilians in plain clothes. At one point, a tour group even passed through, their guide pointing out the vastness of the facility and the elite Triangle squadron, which flew to points all over the world in minutes.

Once Grey thought she spotted Jet, and her heart leapt. But when the man in the dark coat turned around, she saw it wasn't him. Would they dare to kill the emperor's son? She cringed at the thought. It would be her fault if they did, and she already had one man's blood on her hands.

Finally, Yurkutz and her entourage returned. Grey backed up against the wall as the door unlocked, and a female drone stepped inside. Her face was covered in dark bioskin, but the back of her skull was metallic.

"Bind her hands in front," the general said to the drone. Then to Grey she warned, "Don't think I will hesitate to terminate you if necessary."

Grey raised her chin. "If you kill me, you will never find my parents."

"Ah, but there's always Rin."

She almost lunged at Yurkutz again, but the drone's fingers gripped her with no mercy.

The general laughed. "You Alexanders certainly have little regard for self-preservation. That will be your undoing, I'm afraid."

They walked across the hangar, passed through another guarded entrance, and headed down a hallway until they came to a dead end. General Yurkutz faced the wall for several seconds, and Grey guessed it was scanning her features. An automatic door silently bisected the wall, and they walked through.

This space was double the size of the last one. In the

center was a class of cosmoship Grey had never seen before. Black and cylindrical, every facet of its surface gleamed. There were no windows or doors visible on its hull.

The vessel was heavily guarded, and Grey saw drones standing as still as cacti along the entire perimeter of the hangar. She paused briefly until the drone behind her shoved her toward the ship. That same claustrophobic feeling she'd felt when she'd passed under the border fence wire and when Carr had locked the door behind them began to press in on her, and Grey resisted, planting her feet on the white cement floor.

"Where are you taking me?" Her voice sounded shrill.

The drone grabbed her by both arms, and this time she kicked back, hitting its armored leg with her boot. The drone tightened its grip. It felt like she was being held by a huge pair of pliers.

With firm, pointy fingers, the general gripped Grey by the hair and yanked her face upward. Staring into the woman's golden eyes, Grey read the silent, murderous threat.

"Shall we proceed?" Fingernails dug into Grey's scalp.

Grey winced. She had no choice. They walked her up and into the black ship, and that's when Grey knew for sure she'd never see her sister again.

The muscles in Grey's legs ached as her captors led her through the bowels of the cosmoship. It had to be at least twenty times the size of the craft sitting dormant in their silo, larger than anything she'd ever read about.

In what appeared to be the center of the vessel, she spotted four hulking redflare cannons, which looked powerful enough to blow a hole through a building, and crate after crate of supplies. Some were labeled, most were not, but there were enough to supply an army.

Where were they headed?

They took her through a luxurious lounge, and Grey squinted at the room's sudden bright light. Clusters of thick, white leather chairs were parked around tables with the Mazdaar emblem decoratively carved into their surfaces. Magnetic grooves in the tables would hold cups and plates during flight.

A shiny bar, stocked with hundreds of gleaming, colorful

bottles filled one wall, and she guessed the other wall could be transformed into a viewing screen for entertainment.

The man who'd greeted them in the first hangar approached.

"Captain Hertzog," Yurkutz said, her voice taking on a slightly respectful tone. Was it because she was now in his domain?

"General Yurkutz," he said. "I trust you have found things to be satisfactory?"

She gave him a curt nod.

Hertzog eyed Grey, his gaze resting on her restraints. "Are those really necessary?"

"Not negotiable."

"The passengers will notice."

"Let them."

Grey saw something spark in the pilot's eyes. He raised his brow and lowered his voice. "This is my ship, General."

"So do your job," she snapped, ushering Grey to a cluster of five chairs in the corner. "We will stay out of your way."

Yurkutz pushed Grey down into one of them, and she collapsed into the cushions.

"I will return shortly," she said, and with a flick of her eyes she seemed to telepathically order the larger of the drones to sit in the seat across from Grey. She left the room with Captain Hertzog, trailed by the remaining drone pair.

Grey didn't bother trying to talk to her guard. The intelligence of a drone could sometimes be equivalent to that of a human, but she'd never be able to have a conversation with one. This machine had no idea what fear felt like. Or love.

She covered her face with her tied hands, trying to keep from crying. She wished she believed in a god she could pray to. Mom and Dad had. She had too, once.

If I go up to the heavens, you are there.

This time, Grey let the verse linger in her mind. She would fight to keep from revealing anything about Rin or her parents, but how long could she withstand torture? Maybe prayer would give her some strength. She'd heard about condemned men dying with a smile on their lips because of faith in their deity.

If there is a god, could you please show yourself to me?

Grey arranged her hands in her lap and tried to relax into the soft chair. Mom and Dad had taught them about how things used to be, about the freedom people had enjoyed before Mazdaar.

When Mazdaar took control, they had promised a greater freedom, the privilege of belonging to an enlightened society, and the comfort of being taken care of. That sense of security lured most. Dad used to say it was human nature to, in times of crisis, sign over one's rights in exchange for it. The problem was that with security came complacency. And that was worse than death, Dad had said.

A deep, almost imperceptible, vibration came from somewhere beneath Grey's feet, and she felt herself breathing faster. They'd started the engines.

In an attempt to keep herself calm, Grey counted the chairs. Eighty-four.

Evangeline Yurkutz returned. Behind her was a group of passengers dressed in garb from all corners of the world. They filed in as the general took her place in a chair beside Grey. A few of the younger men headed straight for the bar. One couple holding hands strolled toward some chairs at the far end of the room and began caressing as if they were alone.

But everyone who entered eventually noticed Grey. Their gaze would inevitably fall on her bound hands, and they'd either quickly look away and pretend they hadn't seen her or show a look of disdain before doing so.

Only one passenger did not look away. His closely

cropped Afro-textured hair and mustache were white, but his eyebrows remained even darker than his skin. He stood out as the only member of the group who appeared over sixty. He seated himself in the chair on the other side of Grey and smiled at her. For some reason, he didn't seem to care that she was sitting with the head of the Mazdaar High Council.

Soon the room hummed like a party. Drinks were poured, toasts given, and laughter punctuated the air. Who were these people, and where were they all going?

Suddenly all the lights went out, the only illumination coming from the bar where the counter and stools were outlined in blue light. A rush of music flooded the room, the beat thumping in Grey's ears.

As one, the people let out a deafening roar of excitement accompanied by whistles and cheers. They seemed to know what was coming next.

"Don't even think about talking to anyone," General Yurkutz said.

"Welcome, adventurers!" A speaker boomed, and Grey cringed at the decibel level. "You are about to embark on the trip of a lifetime!"

More whoops and hollers.

"Each one of you is to be commended for your enthusiasm and incredible bravery to travel where no modern man or woman has traveled before! You have been selected from a pool of millions to journey to the stars! Welcome to *Genesis*! Please be seated."

A thunder of applause filled the room. Grey could see the forms of people heading for their seats.

Adventurers?

The lights came up, and Grey felt the vibration increasing under her feet. The white-haired man turned as if to speak to her.

"Well, young—"

"You will not speak to the prisoner."

"And pray do tell, why not?"

"For your safety, sir."

"My name is Dr. Henry Lenoir," he said, "and I don't see anything about this girl that would jeopardize my well being."

Evangeline Yurkutz stood, all six feet of her towering over the old man. Grey silently begged him to shut up so he wouldn't be hurt, but if he was intimidated he didn't show it. Instead, he calmly looked up from his seat at her.

"Ma'am . . ." A steward in a crisp, flight suit approached them. "You need to sit down for takeoff."

Yurkutz whirled at the steward. "Do you know who I am?"

"I don't care who you are. You're on this flight, and you're my responsibility. Please sit down."

Grey stared down at her hands, waiting for the general's wrath to boil over, but instead she marched past the steward and toward the door where the captain had disappeared earlier. The steward ran after her.

"You will take me to Hertzog," Yurkutz said.

Dr. Lenoir smiled. "Well, we have a moment, at least."

"She's right," Grey said.

"Oh?"

"If you talk to me, you really could be in danger."

He laughed. "I'm willing to take the risk."

Grey held up her manacled hands to emphasize her words. "She wouldn't hesitate to kill you if you got in her way."

"Not on this ship." Dr. Lenoir reached for her wrists, and she noted the contrast of his ebony skin next to her own.

She pulled away, but he gently touched her where the blood had pooled under the surface and her skin was rubbed raw.

"I'm the ship's doctor," he said. "Once we pass through the Tunguska tunnel I can help you with these wounds."

"I doubt she'll let you," Grey said.

"Perhaps you don't understand." Dr. Lenoir let her hands go and leaned back in his chair. "Cosmoship *Genesis* is a sovereign entity. Mazdaar may own us on the ground, but once we're in the air . . ." he snapped his fingers. "Captain's orders are law. And since the captain is my son-in-law, I think we can arrange to transfer you to the sick bay for a little while. My wife's on call there now."

She managed a slight smile. "How long will we be in the air?"

"It should be at least two days before we reach Jupiter."

Grey shot him a look. "Jupiter? This ship is going to Jupiter?"

He chuckled. "Why, yes, of course."

15

Mrs. March led Rin through every level of the ship, from the cargo hold to the galley. When she brought her onto the bridge, Rin actually gasped. Every switch, lever, and screen glowed with a faint green light.

"I keyed up the basic power drives," Mrs. March said. "I'm pleased to say just about everything appears to be in working order, thanks to your father."

Four high-backed chairs with the Yien Dynasty's yellow rising sun emblem embroidered in the fabric faced the main panels on a wall Rin guessed became the pilot's windshield. She felt as if she was encroaching on something sacred.

"Amazing," Rin whispered.

"Yes, definitely." Mrs. March dropped into the largest chair and ran her fingers across screen after screen. Lights got brighter, some turned yellow, and a few blinked out.

The commander lifted out her medallion controller. Jet's face appeared in front of her.

"Go ahead," Mrs. March said, fingers still flying across the panels.

When Jet didn't respond right away, Mrs. March eyed the screen, and even Rin could see his eyebrows knit together.

"We have lost her," Jet said.

"What?"

"Yurkutz got to her before I could remove her from lockup."

Rin rushed over. She started to yell questions, but Mrs. March held her back.

"Explain."

"They took her on board *Genesis*."

Mrs. March froze, closing her eyes. "Are you sure?"

"Unfortunately, yes."

"No chance of getting on that ship yourself?"

"They would never allow it. I tried to send one of my men, but it's heavily guarded."

"When is departure?"

"It is gone already."

"We will proceed with the plan. Thank you for letting me know, Jet."

He gave a slight nod.

Rin grabbed Mrs. March's arm. "Where are they taking her?"

The screen went black, and Mrs. March sighed. "Cosmo-ship *Genesis* is Mazdaar's first commercial flight to Jupiter."

An involuntary wail escaped her lips, and Rin gasped for air. "They're taking her to *Jupiter*?"

Mrs. March swiveled her chair back to the panels, talking as she worked. "Another reason why I must expedite Operation Noah. If Mazdaar establishes a foothold on the planet, our plans will be for naught."

Dropping to her knees beside Mrs. March's chair, Rin

looked up at her. Her voice was trembling. "Can you . . . save her?"

Mrs. March stopped her work momentarily and took Rin's hands in hers, looking deep into her eyes. "We will do everything we can."

Grey hadn't known what to expect during takeoff. She'd never flown in anything until the smaller catchship had taken her to Mazdaar City, and that was a transatlantic flight, not a transgalactic expedition.

Pressure grew in her ears, but even as Dr. Lenoir assured her everything was normal, Grey shut her eyes. She was a prisoner in a cosmoship heading for another planet that many scientists still believed was uninhabitable. No one knew where she was. How would she ever get back home now?

"We should be entering the tunnel shortly," Dr. Lenoir told her quietly.

He explained that with the discovery of space tunnels connecting specific points in the universe, a year-long trip to Jupiter could be accomplished in a matter of days. Tunguska was the name they'd given this tunnel connecting the two planets.

Once scientists harnessed the massive energy of the tunnels, everything about space travel changed. It took engineers a generation before they discovered the alloys necessary to build a vessel that could withstand the rigors of the space tunnels, and even cosmoships specifically made for the journey could usually only make a dozen flights before they had to be rebuilt.

His voice calmed her as she tried to focus on his words.

"Tunguska lies directly over our moon's Mare Crisium," Dr. Lenoir went on.

Grey listened but didn't acknowledge him for fear of General Yurkutz. She wondered when the captain would make some kind of announcement. Everyone else in the room seemed distracted, and she guessed they had routed their Dots into the ship's onboard network. She wondered why Dr. Lenoir wasn't doing the same.

When they actually entered the tunnel, it was without any warning. One moment Grey was sitting in her chair trying to calm her nerves; the next, she couldn't move. The force was so intense it pushed every part of her body into the seat. She could almost feel her internal organs compressing. A whine at a frequency so high she could only hear it inside her head reverberated and made her feel like she was going insane.

Cosmoships had countering systems to cut down on the G forces and noise, but if this was what it felt like with them on, she could only imagine their intensity. Grey couldn't help but imagine the ship breaking into pieces, and her with it.

Just as she began to taste blood, the pressure suddenly ceased and she was able to fill her lungs again.

"We'll travel normally the rest of the way," Dr. Lenoir said, wiping his forehead with a handkerchief. "It's still a two-day journey ahead, but we've crossed the threshold. Tunguska gives us a huge leg up."

When the captain announced that the passengers were free to enjoy the lounge and unfasten their seat restraints, Grey stared down at her bound hands, knowing she wasn't going to be getting up. What did Mazdaar have planned for her on Jupiter? She tried to recall everything Mrs. March had said about the planet, but her thinking seemed fuzzy. Had the pressure damaged her nervous system?

General Yurkutz returned, and for a moment Grey thought she would pass by and leave her alone with Dr. Lenoir. But the drone guarding her pulled her out of her seat. She didn't even have time to say good-bye to Dr. Lenoir before she was once again led off, following the general.

The drone herded Grey from the lounge area back down into the bowels of the ship. They descended two flights of stairs and passed numerous uniformed guards before reaching a room that opened with a scan of Yurkutz's facial features.

When Grey saw what was inside, she shrunk back. The room was packed with Mazdaar military. She had thought this was a civilian flight.

They passed through the room and down a narrow corridor. Grey soon lost track of which way was out. All she knew was that she ended up in an interrogation chamber, sitting on a chair with her hands still bound. The light was so bright she was squinting.

General Yurkutz stood in front of her, arms crossed.

"We will begin now," she said, the intensity of her gaze causing Grey to cower inwardly.

"I've told you I don't know where they—"

The shock hit before she could finish her sentence, and Grey gritted her teeth against the voltage.

"I will ask you a question, and you will answer," Yurkutz said.

Grey nodded her head erratically, and the shock let up.

"Were your parents working for the Yien Dynasty?"

She said nothing.

Yurkutz rolled her eyes. "Even if you thought they were dead, you must know something. Sooner or later, you will realize this front you insist on keeping up will get you nowhere."

She stared at the floor.

"I asked you a question, Grey Alexander."

"They were working for themselves," she muttered through her teeth.

"Themselves?"

With a jerk of Yurkutz's eyes, a life-size hologram appeared in the room. The image looked so realistic, Grey almost believed Jet was actually standing in front of her. But holograms always had a slightly translucent quality if you knew what to look for, especially around the extremities. At Jet's feet, she spotted the fuzzy anomalies in the image.

"Who is this man?"

That was an odd question. Yurkutz already knew who he was.

"Jet Yien."

"Is it true you have sold him illegal contraband?"

Not wanting to incriminate Jet, she decided to lie. "No."

"No?" Yurkutz's voice became hard.

"You heard me."

The Mazdaar general's pupils seemed to narrow in frustration, and it gave Grey a moment of satisfaction.

The hologram quickly dissolved, another taking its place. Rin.

"And who might this be?"

Grey tried not to let her horror show.

"What a shame for her to lose both her parents and her only sister, don't you think?"

"I'm not lost yet."

Yurkutz laughed, and the sound sent a shiver up Grey's spine. She kept her eyes on the image of Rin, wondering how they'd gotten it. A silly grin was spread across her sister's face. She was dressed in camo, like they'd worn to Jet's hideout. Was this taken at Jet's?

"Miss her?"

She wouldn't answer that.

Leaning down close to her face, Evangeline Yurkutz seemed to study her like she was a specimen in an experiment.

Maybe she was.

"They wouldn't have told you much, but still . . . what do you know about Operation Noah?"

Grey wished the name did mean something to her. She wished she had some kind of information to give that would buy her some time.

"Nothing," she finally said.

"Wrong answer."

This time Grey screamed as the current surged through her body.

16

"You have a decision to make," Mrs. March said, stepping back onto the scaffolding.

Rin followed her, still in a state of shock. How could her sister be on her way to Jupiter? Why would Mazdaar even want her there?

Mrs. March gestured down the corridor, beyond which lay everything Rin had ever known. "I know this is your home," Mrs. March said, "but I don't believe you're safe here anymore."

"I have to leave, don't I?"

Mrs. March's expression was kind. "I promised your parents I'd look out for you girls. Any time now, Mazdaar could choose to decimate the Preserve and flush people like me from hiding, and I don't want you to get caught in the crossfire."

"I don't care about me." Rin smacked the palm of her hand against the wall. "They have my sister, and I've got to do something!"

"We can evacuate you to someplace safe."

Rin could still see her sister standing out on that bluff, allowing them to take her without a fight. She knew why Grey hadn't run—it was to protect *her*. What kind of sister would she be if she didn't at least try to rescue her?

Mrs. March was right. She did have a decision to make, and it was one Rin had no trouble making. She'd never forgive herself if she hid somewhere safe while Grey was in danger.

Rin faced Mrs. March. "They're really taking her to Jupiter?"

"Yes."

"And you're going there too?"

"Yes."

"Then I'm coming with you." She quickly brushed past her and opened the door that led back to her father's workshop.

"I was hoping you'd say that."

Everything looked different now. Every tool, each piece of equipment her father had bartered for, the rolls of wire sitting in a neat row—they had a purpose. All these years, she'd thought Dad just loved to tinker, and instead he'd been down here working on something of great importance. Something to save their family. She pictured Dad hunched over one of the tables working late into the night. Had she been so young she hadn't noticed his attention to the cosmoship? She knew it was there, but he had never really talked about it.

"What will they do when they realize Grey doesn't have any information?" Rin asked.

Mrs. March gave her a quick sideways hug. "That's what worries me."

"They'll have no use for her then, will they?"

"Perhaps there is another possibility."

Rin had seen Evangeline Yurkutz's calculating yellow eyes

once before. Even in a hologram they glowed with a thirst for power. Rin was sure that woman wouldn't hesitate to kill someone who got in her way.

They climbed the circular steps to the living quarters, Rin leading the way. She turned back toward Mrs. March. "What other possibility?"

"It's just speculation."

"Tell me."

With a long sigh, Mrs. March wiped her dirty hands on her pants. Her fingers left smudges in the denim fabric. "They could use her to bait your parents."

Grey must've blacked out during the interrogation. She woke up in a cell like the one where she'd been held in Mazdaar City, and the slab of a bed was just as hard and uncomfortable.

She clutched at the flimsy blanket lying on top of her body. Her sweat-soaked shirt had dried stiff against her skin, and she could smell how dirty she was becoming. At least they'd removed the restraints. They couldn't shock her without them. Not unless they'd developed some new kind of technology.

She almost laughed at the absurdity of that thought. She was flying in a cosmoship to Jupiter. They no doubt had technology she couldn't even fathom. Yet as far as she knew, they hadn't developed a way to read unconnected minds without inserting sensors.

A wave of fear crashed over Grey. What if they'd implanted something in her brain while she was unconscious? Being unconnected was the only thing she had in her favor. If she could stay unconnected, they could never know everything.

When the cell door opened and an androgynous drone pulled her off the bed, her legs gave out and she fell. She'd promised herself she would never beg, but down on her knees, Grey could only speak one word.

"Please . . ."

Grabbing her with both metallic hands, the drone forced her to stand. Hanging from its belt were the restraints. It snapped them onto her wrists, pulling each arm behind her back.

"You will come with me," the drone said in a monotone voice.

Down the dreaded hallway they went, and Grey tried to prepare herself for what was ahead. How long could she withstand torture? How bad would it get?

So far General Yurkutz's power of persuasion had been limited to shocks. Debilitating and painful, yet she knew there were other ways to make people talk. Ways that left worse scars.

They turned a corner, and Grey couldn't help thinking of Rin. She hoped her sister would not despair and would believe that Grey would do everything in her power to come back, but her own hope of escape was fading with every step. The drone approached a wall where a door quickly materialized. It slid open, and a slender, older African woman dressed in medical scrubs was waiting. Silver hoop earrings the size of her hand hung from her earlobes. She looked at Grey and smiled.

"Come in, sweetheart," she said.

Grey hesitated for a moment before the drone poked her in the back. This looked like a sick ward. An examination table along the far wall was illuminated with bright lights. Five cots separated by curtains lined the other wall.

The woman acted as if she'd been expecting her and led her to a chair by the examination table.

"That will be all," she said to the drone, and it turned and walked out.

Grey stared after its broad back.

"Dr. Lenoir sent the drone to get you."

"But . . ."

The woman smiled again. "General Yurkutz isn't the only one with authority on this ship." Her smile disappeared when she looked Grey up and down. "My word, child. What have they done to you?"

Grey dropped into the chair. "As I told Dr. Lenoir, you're only asking for trouble if you help me. Yurkutz is going to find out where I am."

"We are aware of that."

Dr. Henry Lenoir appeared from behind one of the curtain partitions. He now wore the pale-green lab coat of a doctor.

"I was just telling your patient here that you'll be taking care of her," the woman said.

"Thank you, Tessa," Dr. Lenoir said. "This is my wife and nurse. Now, young lady, I don't believe I've had the pleasure of knowing your name."

"Grey." She studied the couple standing before her. They had to be wondering why she was a prisoner. "Why are you doing this for me?"

"How old are you?" Dr. Lenoir ignored her question.

"Seventeen."

Tessa sighed. "We have grandchildren your age back home with our daughter."

"And we took an oath when we entered our professions to 'come for the benefit of the sick.'" Dr. Lenoir reached for Grey's hands, producing a small tool that looked like a fork on one end but was flat metal on the other. With one click to her restraints, they fell from her wrists. "That includes you."

Now that the restraints were removed, the bright examination light revealed how deep her wounds had become.

Dr. Lenoir examined them, touching the skin around the

gouges, and she winced. In unison, doctor and nurse shook their heads.

"Are you feeling nauseous?" Dr. Lenoir asked.

She nodded.

"You're a strong girl. I've treated men twice your age who received half the voltage you've received, and they were barely lucid."

Grey nervously glanced at the door, half expecting General Yurkutz to barge in and drag her away.

"Don't worry." Dr. Lenoir smiled. "General Yurkutz won't be able to override the recommendation of the ship's doctor. Now, let's clean you up. Would you care to lie down?"

Grey eyed one of the cots, and her eyes drooped at the thought of resting.

"I thought so." Dr. Lenoir helped her up, and with Tessa on her other side, they led Grey over to the cot. She groaned as she stretched out on the surprisingly-comfortable mattress that contoured to her body, hugging her with soft warmth.

"You'll find the pain will gradually subside now," Dr. Lenoir said. "The cot is made of a healing silica."

Nurse Tessa sat down beside the bed and began typing in the air on a virtual keyboard.

"Do you have to enter this in the system?" Grey asked.

"Your personal data won't be mentioned," Tessa said. "But every patient we catalogue gives us one more piece in the puzzle of the human body and allows us to help others in the future."

Dr. Lenoir cleared his throat. "Please note first that the patient has deep lacerations, as well as erythema and ecchymosis circumferentially around both wrists. Please also note there are second-degree burns from numerous macro-shocks, and the patient seems to be suffering secondary effects from the electrical current."

Grey closed her eyes as the doctor cleaned the wounds on her wrists and spread a thin layer of an ointment that felt like it flowed through her skin and soothed her flesh straight to the bones.

She opened her eyes when she felt him press a metallic disc to her chest.

"What's that?"

"I'm taking your vitals." Dr. Lenoir blinked his eyes shut momentarily, and she pictured her heart rate, oxygen level, and a million other statistics scrolling across his vision field in little red numbers and text.

Dr. Lenoir let out a small *hmm*.

Grey watched the doctor work. At one point she saw him pique an eyebrow, but other than that she had no idea whether his read on her was good or bad. After a minute, he removed the disc from her chest and slipped it into the breast pocket of his coat.

"That explains a few things," he said.

"What?"

"You're not connected."

Tessa lifted her eyes to her husband's, then kept typing.

Grey suddenly felt exposed lying on the cot, and she moved to sit up.

Dr. Lenoir gently pressed her back down. "You are safe here. Don't worry."

Grey stared up at the ceiling, relieved Mazdaar hadn't yet violated her by forcing her to connect. "I won't do it."

"It's a painless procedure."

"That's not it." She thought back to everything her parents had ever told her about Mazdaar's plans to manipulate those who connected. It wouldn't start right away, they'd said. It might even take years, but it would come. Her family had risked everything to evade connection. Now it was happening to her.

"You don't have to explain," Dr. Lenoir said.

"I just don't want to connect," she said.

"That's quite obvious."

"Are you going to make me?"

"No. That does not concern us."

Grey closed her eyes. Maybe not, but she knew sooner or later it would concern Evangeline Yurkutz. And the general *could* make her connect.

17

The motion siren wailed as Rin and Mrs. March were busy inventorying food supplies. Rin's adrenaline kicked into overdrive. The silo's motion alarms each had a different tone to indicate where the breach in the system was located. This one was coming from the emergency exit up on the bluff. The sensors were "smart" and could usually distinguish between human and animal.

They jogged into the control room and checked the security screens. Mrs. March maximized the camera positioned on the bluff. Several human figures came into view.

"We have a few weapons," Rin said, hating the thought of holding one. She'd always trusted Grey to protect them and hoped she'd never be forced to shoot anything.

"It won't be necessary." Mrs. March zoomed in on the figures standing at the exit and keyed on the audio. "Identify yourselves," she said.

"Sergeant Rooley, Commander," a male voice answered.

"And my family. We received your transmission."

The man turned his head, and Rin almost gasped when she realized it was Kildare Rooley, the man Grey often traded with. The man with the tigers. As if for emphasis, a low growl came through the speakers.

With a chuckle, Mrs. March pressed the button to unlock the doors. "I'm hearing more than your family, Sergeant."

"Can't leave 'em behind," he said.

Mrs. March turned to Rin. "I've called up reinforcements. We'll need more than you and me for this mission."

"He works for you?"

"That's why I often urged Grey to trade with him."

Rin shook her head. It felt like the silo was being invaded, and that went against everything she'd ever known.

Mrs. March gave her an encouraging smile. "Trust me."

For the rest of the day, Rin was forced to watch her quiet home transformed into the command center of the Yien Dynasty's Special Forces. What seemed like a never-ending stream of strangers flooded through the silo, loading crates and packs into the cosmoship and creating such a loud din Rin could barely think straight.

Unable to eat supper later that evening, Rin found Mrs. March and four others hunched over a table in the middle of her father's workshop. Rin watched the group, leaning up against the cement wall.

"Did you tell them it was imperative they come?" Mrs. March had both hands on the table.

"They have refused," Kildare said.

Mrs. March rubbed her eyes and sighed.

"Unfortunately, they have grown complacent," said a woman Rin had never seen before. She was younger than Mrs. March but old enough to be Rin's mother. Freckles splattered her cheeks, and her hair was the color of desert sandstone. Her accent sounded European, but Rin wasn't sure. Where in the Preserve had these people been hiding?

Mrs. March hung her head and whispered, "Dear God, protect them. We have tried."

"Who are you talking about?" Rin stepped forward.

All eyes turned to her.

"Come here," Mrs. March said.

She slowly walked over to the table. Kildare gave her a slight nod, then focused on the ancient maps spread out across the surface. Rin had never seen so much paper in one place.

"Orinda understands our cause and has agreed to join us," Mrs. March said.

"But she's just a child," a man taller than Kildare spoke. He wore a turban, and his dark eyes searched hers. Mrs. March introduced the man as lieutenant Arwin Choudry before addressing his concern.

"Perhaps," she said. "But she is Tanner and Sue Alexander's daughter."

Rin thought she saw something falter on the faces of the four adults standing before her. A hint of reverence passed over their features, and the lieutenant did not press the issue further.

The red-haired woman introduced herself as Communications Specialist Maggie Coronado while a younger woman next to her remained silent. With a single braid draped across her shoulder, she eyed Rin like she was an annoying mosquito.

"And this is Dana."

With a dismissive nod, Dana kept her focus on Mrs. March. Rin noticed she had been introduced without a rank.

"I have asked Dana to head the effort to rescue Grey. She has intimate knowledge of Mazdaar and especially General Yurkutz." Mrs. March gestured to Dana. "Will you share with Rin why you are best qualified for this endeavor?"

Stepping closer to the table, Dana clasped her hands in front of herself. "General Yurkutz will stop at nothing to have her way." Her voice was low and matter of fact. "She is especially intent on finding your parents."

"But . . . why?" Rin shook her head. "Why are my parents so important to Mazdaar?"

Mrs. March shuffled through the papers. "Your father is a great scientist, Rin. When he was just a young man barely older than Grey is now, he was working on a project to develop hybrid insect MEMS. Instead, he accidentally discovered the technology Mazdaar needed to create drones from human bodies."

"What?"

"They were made strictly of synthetic material until this century," Dana added. "Then, with so many war casualties, bodies were in abundance and parts were harvested and banked."

Rin shuddered.

"But body parts only got them so far. Mazdaar has tried for years to create a drone from an intact human body," Dana continued.

Rin held up her hand. "Why?"

"Building a drone isn't cheap." Mrs. March stared down at the table. "And while they can withstand much abuse on the battlefield, once they're broken they aren't easy to fix."

Dana's expression remained grim. "Mazdaar projected that if there was a way to preserve a human body and use its brain to send messages to its limbs, it could become the perfect soldier. No objections, no emotions. And if it was irreparably damaged in battle, it could be discarded and another would take its place. They would be more expendable."

"Your father," Mrs. March said, "invented the chips that mimic the signals of the human brain. They're called Gihern chips. He did not know Mazdaar intended to use them in the way they did. When he found out, he destroyed his research, the prototypes, everything. That's reason number one that they want your parents."

With a small sigh, Dana placed her hand on the nearest map, tracing some lines with her finger. "Evangeline also has a personal vendetta against them."

Rin could feel herself becoming totally overwhelmed.

"In a way, I'm responsible." Dana's voice dropped to almost a whisper. "Your parents are part of the reason why I am not following in Evangeline's footsteps."

Mrs. March slid a chair out for Rin. "A year before they disappeared, they were part of the team who helped Dana defect from the system."

Rin studied Dana. She was probably only a few years older than Grey, but there was something about her that made her seem older. Like she'd seen the underbelly of the world and survived. "Why would Evangeline care so much about you defecting?"

Dana paused, not meeting Rin's eyes. "Because Evangeline Yurkutz is my mother."

Grey couldn't remember Dr. Lenoir sending her back to her cell. He must have given her a sleep aid, because she was sure she'd been out for hours. Maybe the relief from the pain in her wrists and arms helped too. When she did open her eyes, she noticed another bowl of mashed meal on the floor of her cell.

This time Grey didn't eat it. The nourishment wasn't worth the stomach ache.

A drone came for her not long after she woke up, and Grey didn't struggle as her hands were bound again. For now there was no escape, but her time with Dr. Lenoir and Tessa had given her a glint of hope that not everyone under Mazdaar rule was like General Yurkutz.

The drone led her back up to the lounge and deposited her in the same seat she'd occupied during takeoff and sat down beside her. Apparently others had gotten the memo to converge too, because the room was packed.

She didn't see Dr. Lenoir. Or General Yurkutz.

The passengers talked among themselves but kept looking around the room as if waiting for someone or something. After almost an hour, their whispers morphed into grumbles.

A young man close to her age plopped down in the empty seat on her left. Stubble dotted his chin, and his hair was shorn on the sides but long and wavy on the top.

Shifting in her seat, Grey tried to get comfortable but caught the guy glancing at her bound hands. She leaned back and closed her eyes. At least they were less likely to hurt her out here in this public space.

"What'd you do?"

Grey flipped her eyes open but didn't bother looking at the guy beside her.

"I said what'd you do?"

She lifted her manacled hands. "Does it matter?"

"You kill somebody?"

Grey dropped them back in her lap. "Why are *you* here?"

He laughed. "*Genesis* is the greatest chance of a lifetime." He spread his arms as if indicating the whole universe. "Some grads go to Paris or Berlin for their studies, but I, Paul Alvarez III, am going to Jupiter. Can you believe that?"

Remembering the drone beside her, Grey tried to tune the young man out. Would there be a way to escape once they landed? On Earth, drones had unlimited range. Communication signals could be repeated through any of the hundreds of Mazdaar satellites. But maybe they had limits on Jupiter.

"I said can you believe that?" Paul was leaning forward, trying to catch her eye.

Grey reluctantly turned to her fellow passenger. She was already in trouble. She didn't need to pretend she was anything but a rebel. "If Mazdaar's so great, why did they tell us Jupiter was uninhabitable for so many years?"

Paul lifted an eyebrow, leaning back into his seat without answering.

"Why'd you want to go?" Grey asked.

"Who wouldn't?" Paul shrugged. "Like I said, it's *the* chance of a lifetime!"

Grey sighed, trying to ignore the pinch of her restraints.

Paul snorted. "Well, maybe not for you."

"No." She glared at him. "Not for me."

Just then a booming announcement came from the speakers, this time without musical fanfare. The male voice—Grey wasn't sure if it was the captain or not—was monotone. "We apologize for the wait, but we think you'll agree it was worth it."

There was a long pause. Then all the lights cut out, and the room was thrust into complete darkness. Not even the blue bar lights remained lit.

A collective gasp spread through the compartment. Grey was wondering how she could take advantage of the darkness when the walls of the ship seemed to disappear and become as glass. In every direction was space. And stars. Magnificent, brilliant, stars.

Even more amazing was a sight Grey could barely believe she was seeing. Suspended in the darkness, surrounded by the stars and filling the entire right window, was an enormous planet bathed in swirling bands of color—vibrant reds and oranges, blues and greens.

Someone whispered, "Oh, my word."

Jupiter.

19

As Jupiter loomed, reflecting light on everything in the lounge, the passengers murmured excitedly. Everyone pointed and whispered, but Grey could only stare at the massive planet where her life might come to an end.

They'd be landing soon. How long would General Yurkutz find it useful to keep her alive? She hadn't given them any information. Why keep an informant who didn't inform?

"We hope you enjoy the rest of your flight," the voice finished as the lights switched back on.

The windows disappeared, and the walls manifested again. Conversations resumed, and that's when Grey spotted Yurkutz sauntering into the lounge from the direction of the captain's quarters. Her cape fluttered behind her in a wake and two drones trailed her, both wearing armored breastplates and leg and arm shields.

Rising at her approach, Grey's drone guard gave a salute like it had been programmed to do.

Grey remained slumped in her chair.

"Bring her," Yurkutz ordered, and Grey was pulled up to standing. She jerked out of the drone's grasp and followed, struggling to keep up. Would this be another torture session?

The tiny chamber they took her to had a panel of controls on one wall but no chairs or furniture of any kind. As the door closed behind them, Grey felt the heat of fear creeping up her neck. Alone with three drones and General Yurkutz. This couldn't—

"Begin," the general said.

Before Grey could even wonder what that meant, the female drone backhanded her across the face. The blow almost knocked Grey down, but she sidestepped enough to catch herself. Blood instantly flowed from her nose, dripping on the pristine floor. Another punch opened her lip, and she fell to her knees.

"That will do," Yurkutz said, and the drone stepped back.

Her face stinging, Grey raised her eyes to the monster of a woman before her.

"Why don't . . . you believe me? I don't know anything."

Turning from her, Yurkutz maneuvered the controls on the wall, and a video screen materialized in front of them. The Mazdaar general rapidly blinked three times. "Did you know your father hid something very important from you?"

More blood tickled down Grey's chin.

"I knew him before you were ever born," Yurkutz said.

"You're lying."

Was this woman toying with her? Trying to rile her into giving up her parents?

Grey focused on the hovering screen between them. At first all she saw was static; then slowly an image appeared. When she saw the man's worried face she let out an involuntary sob, the horror of Mazdaar's plan sinking in.

"Dad!" Grey climbed to her feet.

The drones instantly surrounded her, holding her back. One of them punched her in the stomach, and Grey doubled over. Was showing her Dad's picture another of Yurkutz's sick torture techniques, or was that a live transmission of her father?

"Good afternoon, Tanner." The general's voice dripped diplomacy. "You are wise to finally respond to our requests for communication."

"I want to see my daughter."

"You will, sir. You most definitely will."

"What have you done to her?"

"It's good to see you are alive and well. Rumors of your death have been greatly exaggerated."

His sandy hair was grayer and he now had a full beard, but Grey would recognize Dad anywhere. Could it really be him? If so, where was he? And where was Mom?

"I refuse to speak further until I see my daughter," Tanner said.

General Yurkutz smiled. "Very well."

Rin had been watching Communications Specialist Maggie Coronado program the computer on the cosmoship's main bridge all morning. Apparently, the CS had been living ten miles from the silo in an underground bunker for longer than Rin had been alive.

Rin was getting tired of waiting. "Ms. Coronado, what exactly are you doing?"

Wearing an auris plug, the woman had been tapping on a keyboard, studying screens, and listening intently through her device for hours. "Please call me Maggie."

"Okay, Maggie, what are you doing?"

"These holographic receivers need to be tuned." Maggie

pressed her bracelet controller with a fingertip. "And I'm transferring the alert codes from my controller to the ship. If anyone from Mazdaar as much as sneezes about Jupiter, we'll know it."

Rin sat down on the cold, metal floor. Mrs. March had assigned her to help Maggie, but she'd been doing nothing but standing around. She wondered if they were just trying to keep her out of the way.

"Will there be others coming?" So far, about thirty people had arrived in the silo, but Rin knew there were hundreds living in the Preserve.

Maggie pushed strands of her curly hair away from her face. "Commander March made the call to evacuate the southern region of the Preserve, but not everyone responded."

"Why not?"

Maggie gave a sad shrug. "Perhaps they forgot we have an enemy. They've been lulled into complacency over the years."

Pulling her knees to her chest, Rin rested her chin on them.

God, if you're out there, I need your help. And please help Grey, wherever she is. I want to see her again.

An insistent, high-pitched beep oscillated from one of the receivers. Maggie's hands flew over the knobs and dials. "Whoa. That's a transmission from *Genesis* herself."

She brought up a green, holographic image. The split-screen hovered in midair, disappeared, then hovered again.

Rin clambered to her feet. Maggie was muttering at the controls when Mrs. March, Kildare, and Dana burst into the room.

"We've never received one from this distance before," Maggie said. "I'm hoping the system can handle it."

"Is there audio?" Kildare asked.

"Bringing it online."

"Can they hear *us*?" Rin asked.

"It's one-way. We're tapping into a remote conversation," responded Maggie.

Squinting, Rin tried to make out the faces as the blurry images slowly sharpened. She recognized them both almost simultaneously. One side of the screen showed General Evangeline Yurkutz, a woman Rin was beginning to hate. On the other—Rin clasped her hand to her mouth.

Dad.

"As we suspected," Dana whispered. "They're using Grey to get to Tanner."

Mrs. March came and stood beside Rin as Yurkutz's voice sliced through the room. "Tanner Alexander, I present your daughter, Grey."

They could see the general step back, and the camera zoomed in on Grey surrounded by drones. Her hands were tied, and a stream of blood flowed from her nose down her lip and chin.

Rin cried into her hand.

"She's alive, dear." Mrs. March patted her back. "At least she's alive."

"But what have they done to her?"

Dana stared at the hologram, fingers balled. "Probably electroshock torture and a few old-fashioned punches for Tanner's sake."

Mrs. March shot a look in Dana's direction, but the young woman didn't seem to notice. Her eyes were glued to the screen.

Dad's expression morphed into rage. Then he seemed to suppress his anger and asked, "What do you want?" He pronounced each word slowly and deliberately.

"You know what we want," Yurkutz said. "You have three days. We will be waiting at Orion settlement."

Dana was shaking her head.

"And I don't think I need to remind you . . ." A groan came from somewhere behind her, obviously Grey. "What will happen if you decline our invitation."

Rin could see her father's eyes glistening in the high-def image. Then everything went black. No one moved or spoke until Maggie stood up with a sigh.

"Was that really my father?" Rin whispered.

"I believe so," Mrs. March said.

"And Grey?"

Dana turned around, facing Rin. "She's onboard *Genesis*, which should touch down on Jupiter later today."

"But where was he? How did they contact him?"

Mrs. March gestured toward Maggie. She scrolled through several screens then gave a small nod of finality. "His signal came from the surface."

"What?" Rin shot Mrs. March a questioning look. "He's on *Jupiter*? How can that be?"

"It's certainly possible," Mrs. March said in a low voice. "Last we heard from Tanner and Sue, they were about to hit the Tunguska tunnel." Her eyes met Rin's. "They were on a mission to rescue prisoners from the planet. For years I believed they were dead too. But then we caught wind of Mazdaar's search for them and began to hope."

Rin tried to keep her composure, but she had seen the anguish in her father's eyes and the blood dripping down Grey's face. Yes, they were alive, but for how long? And where was Mom?

20

This time General Yurkutz didn't take Grey back to her cell. Instead, she was marched through the darker, Spartan lounge—the one full of armed Mazdaar military. They were all strapping into their seats. She caught one female soldier staring at her; then the soldier quickly looked away.

One of the drones shoved Grey into a seat in the corner, slipping a chain through her cuffs and attaching it to the chair. Grey pulled at the chain, but it didn't budge.

She tilted her head back to try and stem the flow from her nose, which had started bleeding again. Between the swelling and the blood trickling down the back of her throat, it was hard to breathe. And it was slowly becoming clear why they'd captured her. This wasn't really about her, just like Yurkutz had been saying all along. It was about her parents. For some reason Mazdaar was hunting them down, and Grey was the bait. But how could Dad be on Jupiter?

She wanted to rejoice that he was alive, but Dad would

give in to them. She knew it. He'd come for her, and Yurkutz would capture him too. And where was Mom? Dead?

Please, please, please don't let that be true after all this.

The cosmoship's frame vibrated so violently she had to concentrate to keep her teeth from grinding together. Why had she been separated from the other passengers and brought down here? Her body squashed against her restraints as a roar filled the room. All conversation ceased, and the soldiers braced themselves as much as Grey did. Was that fear in their eyes?

Every fiber in Grey's body seemed to shudder with the ship, and in a matter of seconds the room grew as hot as the desert. It was dangerous to re-enter Earth's atmosphere; it had to be worse on this much larger planet. Would the ship burst into flames and send them all to fiery graves? She was already as good as dead in Mazdaar's hands anyway. Maybe it wouldn't be so terrible to die now. It would be quick, and she wouldn't have to endure any more torment.

Just when Grey thought her ears would burst from the noise, the quaking ceased and the craft seemed to float, her body suspended and light for a moment.

"Men and women of Mazdaar." General Yurkutz's voice came over the loudspeaker. "Prepare for landing as instructed. Proceed according to your orders."

Orders?

In the center of the room, a man with the build of a bear stood up. "All right, you heard her, blokes! This is what you've trained for. I expect you to live up to that emblem you wear!"

The soldiers let out a deafening cheer and sent the two-fingered Mazdaar salute skyward. Grey felt a new sense of dread as a pair of soldiers approached her. They released her from the chair and replaced the shock cuffs with regular handcuffs. For that, at least, she was thankful.

All the uniforms fell into formation two-wide and exited the lounge doors, dragging Grey with them. They marched down multiple corridors until they were back in the bottom hold of *Genesis*, where Grey had first seen the laser cannons. Everyone stood at attention in front of where the hatch doors would no doubt materialize after they settled to the surface of the planet.

It was all Grey could do to shove down her rising panic.

Rin stared up at the gleaming blue cosmoship, *Tevah*. A whisper of steam hissed from its side, white lights glowing along its hull. The sleeping giant was awakening.

Holding Tram's and Trif's lead ropes, Rin felt frozen in place as she took in the magnitude of it all. "Ready, boys?" she whispered.

Trif nudged her arm, but Tram stared at the ship, his ears pointed forward, head raised with apprehension. She tried to ease his tension with a soft voice but knew it would be a long journey for both of them.

She led the zorses toward the jaws of *Tevah*, hoping they wouldn't balk or spook. Tram and Trif had faced many dangers over the years out in the Preserve and were desensitized to strange places and sounds, but this was of a different magnitude entirely. She walked them up the ramp without incident, her boots thumping and their hooves clopping.

Rin tried to act like her older sister and thrust her shoulders back to face this new adventure head on. But she kept seeing the blood on Grey's face, the terror in her eyes. Rin hated Mazdaar for hurting Grey.

She led Tram and Trif into the hold of the vessel. Men and women bustled around her stacking and securing crates, their chatter filling the cavernous space. Someone shouted; someone else called back. Metal clattered on metal, someone hammered, a tiger roared.

Tram and Trif stopped in their tracks at the sound of the predator.

"It's okay," Rin cooed. "It can't get you."

Kildare's cats were safely stowed in cages, along with dozens of other animals, including horses and zebras, dogs and cats. Rin smiled, glad Tram and Trif wouldn't be alone.

Kildare had almost convinced Mrs. March her zorses were expendable since they were sterile, but one look into Rin's horrified face, and Mrs. March had made the exception. Tram and Trif were the only nonbreeding pair of animals allowed on board.

"I hope you realize how privileged you are."

Rin swung around after securing Tram and Trif to see Dana standing behind her. The young woman had changed into a tan, one-piece polymeric flight suit.

"They're . . . I could never . . ."

Dana gave her the hint of a smile. "I know."

Even though she had renounced her mother's name and all its benefits, Dana still carried herself with the poise of a Mazdaar official. Rin had to remember that even though Dana had been connected at birth, she'd had her Dot surgically removed shortly after Mom and Dad helped her escape. There was still a faint white hint of a scar on her forehead where the implant had once been embedded. She certainly seemed loyal enough.

"Could I ask you something?" Dana said.

Rin shrugged.

"How did . . ." Dana glanced away for a moment. "How did you two survive for five years out here by yourselves?"

She wanted to point out that while they might be considered children to Mazdaar and probably to Dana, out here in the

Preserve she and Grey lived as adults. Whether they wanted to or not, they'd grown up fast.

Turning around to watch Trif munching on the dried cactus stems she'd gathered, Rin realized that even though Dana was older than Grey, she was a girl who'd lost her parents too. Rin could hope that someday she might be reunited with her family again, but Dana would never have that.

"We had each other," Rin said.

"If you can make it in the Preserve on your own, you'll get through this."

"I hope so."

Dana started to turn away, but Rin reached for her arm. "Can I ask *you* a question?"

Some of Dana's stony exterior remained, but she nodded.

"Your mother—when she found out you defected, what did she do?"

Dana blinked and jerked her eyes to the right. Maybe it was an old habit from being connected, but it made Rin wish she hadn't asked. How long ago had it happened?

"She put a price on my head," Dana said and then turned around and walked down the ramp.

21

Grey tensed as the ship decelerated, her face still throbbing. "Prepare to move!"

The soldiers gripped their stocky blueflares. They looked like they were capable of burning through walls. Or through a person. She didn't realize she was barely breathing until the outline of the cargo door appeared in front of them. Grey exhaled, trying to calm herself. Touchdown came seconds later, a jolt to her feet. The drone assigned to her tightened its vice-like hold.

"Do not resist," it spoke matter-of-factly.

The door slipped upward on a silent track, and Grey gawked at her first look at Jupiter. A rush of warm, dusty air swirled around them, and for a moment all the humans froze in awe, glancing from the sky to the ground and back. The drones stared straight ahead.

The soil looked like colored marble—shades of yellow, red, and blue swirled together in a kaleidoscope of dust.

Strange, twisted trees with iridescent leaves hulked in the distance. Beyond them were mountains unlike any she'd ever seen. With pointed, vertical rock formations, they looked like a row of massive medieval castles all stretching toward the heavens.

"Move out!"

As one, the Mazdaar army poured from the cosmoship. She labored to keep up while craning to see the sky. Far above the mountains, where on Earth you would expect to see blue, a roiling sea of red and orange clouds writhed and twisted.

"Holy cow," someone muttered.

The skies proclaim the work of His hands.

Grey heard the words in her mother's calm voice, and she could almost see Mom's face and the way she'd stare at a desert sunset with a young Grey at her side. Mom had always loved sunsets.

The drone shoved Grey in the back, shaking away the memory. She focused on keeping her feet moving. Before them stood a massive domed building, very much like something they'd see on Earth. The soldiers rushed toward it, forcing Grey along with them.

Rin stood in the silo's galley and took in everything she'd be leaving behind. Stepping over to the counter, she touched the glass carafe. Even though Grey hated it herself, every morning she heated up water for Rin's cactus tea.

Rin closed her eyes. This was her home. All she'd ever known. What if Mom and Dad came back for her and she wasn't here? And Grey . . . somehow she might free herself from Mazdaar's grip, and then what? Rin knew she'd come here looking for her if she could.

She could leave a note of some kind, but what would she write? *Dear Grey, I'm on Jupiter looking for you.*

"You coming?"

Rin spun towards Dana's bossy voice.

"It's just . . ."

Dana looked around the room, taking in the kitchen. "I left everything behind too."

It did help to know someone understood. And at least Tram and Trif were coming.

"If you're worried about Grey coming back . . ."

Nodding, she took one last look, picturing Grey at the cooling box holding out those strawberries with that silly smile Rin missed so much.

"They won't let her," Dana said. "Not if I know my mother."

Before Rin could respond, an explosive *boom!* rocked the room. Dust floated down from the ceiling, and the lights flickered.

"What was that?" Rin steadied herself against the counter.

Another thunderous jolt shook the floor. Something creaked right above their heads. That wasn't a support girder, was it?

Dana grabbed her by the arm. "Come on!"

Another blast took out the lights.

"What's happening?" The generator should've started up immediately.

"*Now*, Rin!" Dana pulled her into the corridor and down to the silo's lower levels. They felt their way down the stairs and through her father's workshop.

"Bombs," Dana huffed.

"*What?*"

"They found us."

"But the . . . will we still—"

"Hurry!"

By the time Rin and Dana made it into the cavern where

Tevah smoldered, smoke poured from vents in the ship's sides. Its tethers lay in gnarled, metallic heaps, never to be used again. The loading ramp was still down, but by the frantic gestures of the two crew members waiting in the doorway—she couldn't hear a word they said over the engines—Rin guessed she and Dana were the last to board. Energy coursed through her limbs as she and Dana ran up onto the captain's bridge.

"Commander," Dana huffed with a salute as they entered.

"Buckle up, girls. This won't be smooth."

Mrs. March, now dressed in a black flight suit with the Yien Dynasty's emblem on her sleeve, sat in the largest of the seats, her back to them. Maggie and Kildare sat on either side of her, working controls of their own.

"All panels go?" Mrs. March said.

"Go," Kildare responded.

"Main hatch is closed," Maggie said, and Rin noticed a small light in front of her turn from red to green.

Rin quickly dropped herself into a jump seat against the wall. Dana took the one beside her. They were the only civilians allowed on the captain's bridge. Rin still couldn't get over the fact that her mother could've been the pilot in Mrs. March's seat.

Clearly the commander of the entire operation, Rin watched as Mrs. March rushed through a complicated preflight check list, barking at her crew and using words Rin couldn't pronounce.

A muted explosion from somewhere above them shook the cosmoship. Could they still take off? Had anything been damaged?

"Our biggest risk now is those fighter jets outside," Mrs. March muttered.

"Are they after *us*?" Rin asked.

Dana rolled her eyes. "No, they're out there sightseeing."

A rumble crescendoed under Rin's feet. She hadn't ever pictured this ship actually taking off. How could they possibly make it out without damaging *Tevah*?

"Disable shields," Mrs. March said.

The rumble became a roar, and Rin grabbed the noise reducers hanging beside her. She was going to Jupiter. How crazy was that? Had Grey traveled on a ship like this?

"Shields disabled," Maggie responded. Her auburn mane was now tamed with a colorful rag tied around her head.

"Open the roof."

Kildare flipped something on the panel, and several yellow lights blinked on. "Roof open."

"Power at fifty percent," Maggie said.

Leaning toward Rin, Dana had to yell to be heard above the engines or whatever force propelled a ship like this. "This is the most dangerous point. The shields have to be disabled for liftoff."

Rin gripped both armrests.

A screen lit up in front of Kildare, showing what appeared to be a live map of the nearby zones. Several blinking lights dotted the screen.

Rin pictured the ground opening up above them, ready to spew *Tevah* from the underground silo. She felt the ship begin to rise. At first slowly, but within seconds the momentum pushed her down into her seat. Dana gave her a thumbs-up, and she returned it.

A huge windshield materialized in front of Mrs. March and the others, giving them a wide-angle view of the terrain. Rin gasped. They were already soaring above the ridge, so high the massive boulders where she and Grey had hid only yesterday looked like marbles, then like grains of sand. Suddenly, the force of the engines seemed to change. Instead of traveling vertically, the ship now shot across the sky horizontally, like a traditional plane, but at such a high altitude that the sky was dark above them.

"Pretty awesome, huh?" Dana beamed.

Rin was trying not to be sick from the sudden G forces. "How many times have you flown like this?"

"Dozens! I love it."

Rin could barely hear Mrs. March, but she tuned into her voice.

"Shields up?"

"Shields activated," Kildare responded.

"Any movement?"

Maggie scanned her screens. "Not yet."

"Let's keep it that way," Mrs. March said.

Leaning back into her seat, Rin tried to close her eyes, but she couldn't peel her gaze from the view. They were miles above the clouds, but she could still see the patchwork landscape beneath. At this tremendous speed, they were well beyond the Preserve by now.

"Missile lock-on detected," Maggie said as calmly as she'd announced the power levels, and Rin peeked at Dana. The young woman's forehead wrinkled.

"Time?" Mrs. March's profile showed no more concern than Maggie's, but Rin could hear the tension in her voice.

"Thirty," Maggie replied.

That couldn't be good. "A missile's thirty minutes away?"

Shaking her head, Dana watched Mrs. March. "Thirty seconds."

Rin strained to see signs of something deadly out the window, but all she saw was the ground racing below. Was she going to die before she got a chance to help Grey?

"Twenty," Maggie said.

"Prepare for evasion maneuver." Mrs. March's hands hovered over two levers.

"Fifteen."

Rin could feel the speed jamming against her back.

Her eyes focused on the screens, Maggie kept tapping at a panel, and Rin thought she saw a point of light traveling across it.

"Ten," Maggie said.

Kildare gave a nod. "Power, one hundred percent."

"Five."

"Okay, gang." Mrs. March raised her voice. "Hang on!"

Maggie counted off with her fingers the remaining seconds. As she reached one, Rin puked. She could barely turn her head against the sudden impulsion pressing her body.

Rin was so dizzy she could not tell which end was up or down anymore. Commander March spiraled them into a vertical climb, and she thought she saw Dana curl up her nose in disgust as the contents of Rin's stomach now stuck to her flight suit. Still they climbed. Which way was up?

Maggie eyed her screen. "Missile averted."

"Sorry, girls!" Mrs. March said, continuing their climb.

Just when Rin thought she would pass out, the ship seemed to right itself and she let out her breath.

"You thought that was bad," Dana said. "Just wait until we reach Tunguska."

Rin groaned.

22

Grey lost sight of the Jupiter landscape once inside the dome. For how many centuries had mankind assumed this planet was only gases and couldn't support life? Yet here she was standing on its surface, still alive and breathing oxygenated air. Mrs. March was right.

The Mazdaar soldiers herded Grey into a vast, warehouse-like room, depositing her in a cell with no light. She could barely see anything through the slit in the door. The squadrons fell into formation, and the bear-built man she'd seen give orders aboard *Genesis* addressed them.

"Attention!"

All uniforms saluted. "Yes, Major, sir!"

Their shouts bounced off the metallic walls. How long had this building been here? She'd noticed the exterior doors had old-fashioned locks and keys instead of scanners.

"You have been hand-selected for this mission," the major bellowed in a gravelly voice.

Grey stood on tiptoes to see. Why were so many military on this flight in the first place? General Yurkutz couldn't be here just to escort *her*. What danger could be on Jupiter that military was required?

"I have assigned some of you to guard the prisoners; the rest will receive assignments shortly."

Grey's legs suddenly felt shaky.

Prisoners?

"We will bring them in, assign them to cells, and assess their viability."

She tried to look around the room. That's when she noticed that lining the entire perimeter were other cells, some large enough to hold several people.

A sick feeling gripped her when more soldiers marched in from the cosmoship, this time herding the passengers she'd seen in the lounge. The people who'd cheered for their great adventure now looked like frightened antelope.

She saw the love-struck couple who'd been pawing each other now clinging together in fear. Paul was there too, his eyes darting around.

When Grey saw Dr. Lenoir and Tessa in the group, a cry came to her lips. They were being paraded in here like animals. She knew why she was there, but what could this kind couple possibly have done to invoke the wrath of Mazdaar?

The guards crowded the people into a confused huddle in the middle of the room.

"What's going on?" someone shouted. "Where are we?"

Major came forward, a grin plastered on his face. "Welcome to Jupiter!"

A guy Grey had seen earlier hanging out at the bar pushed to the front of the group. "We demand to know what the blazes you're doing with us!"

"Ah," Major said, raising his hand. "A reasonable question."

He snapped his fingers, and two soldiers dragged a struggling man forward.

They flung him to the floor, and Grey flinched. His hands were tied behind his back with shock restraints. That's when she recognized him as the pilot, Captain Hertzog, Dr. Lenoir's son-in-law.

"How dare you," Hertzog said, raising his eyes to the major towering over him. "What authority allows you to treat us like this?"

"Mine," a female voice came from the entrance, and Grey watched General Yurkutz, her ever-present drones shadowing her, march across the cement floor toward the man. Her ubiquitous green uniform cape flowed behind her like smoke.

Climbing to his feet, Hertzog stood in front of her. Sweat dripped down his temple, but he still managed to face the general with defiance. Grey wanted to close her eyes at what it was going to provoke.

"If you think you can defy me," Yurkutz said. "You are terribly wrong."

Hertzog braced. "I am a Mazdaar pilot, and my orders were to fly my ship to Jupiter. I did not agree to imprison these people."

"Well then, sir, you will be an example to all."

General Yurkutz reached into her coat and pulled out a silver object that was shaped like a gun only with a thicker muzzle.

Grey instantly recognized it as an MI pistol. Its charging buzz rang through the room as the general raised it to Hertzog's chest. Grey turned away just as she fired.

The sudden electronic blast reverberated against the walls, quickly followed by a thud. Grey forced herself to look out again. The captain had fallen. Was there any chance it had only been a stun shot?

"No!" someone wailed, and she was almost sure it was Tessa.

Horror and panic spread across the prisoners in a wave. Some screamed; others seemed paralyzed. Yurkutz slowly lowered the MI, its quick succession of electronic beeps telling all that it was recharging. Grey didn't have to look twice to know Hertzog was dead.

"Perhaps now all of you will understand," she said.

A man shoved through the crowd like he was going to make a rush for the general, but two of his companions held him back.

"You killed him!"

Yurkutz slipped the weapon back under her coat. "And I will do the same to anyone else who defies us. We will make this very clear. You are now on the planet Jupiter, and you will die here. How quickly that happens is up to you."

Grey searched the crowd for Dr. Lenoir.

"But where is the settlement we came for?"

With a laugh, Yurkutz waved toward the dome's roof. "This is all the settlement you will know."

Grey remembered again the conversation she'd had with Mrs. March about this evil woman. Were they all going to be killed?

With another wave of her hand, the general ordered the soldiers to disperse the crowd. A few resisters had to be immobilized with derma-rays, and that kept the rest in line. Grey sunk to the floor of her cell, leaning against the wall.

She jumped to her feet again when the door burst open, and two prisoners were shoved into the cell with her.

Dr. Lenoir and Tessa! The door clanged shut behind them.

Grey rushed over and embraced them both. Then Tessa fell to the floor sobbing. Her husband knelt down beside her, stroking her hair. Grey stood helplessly, her heart breaking for them. She didn't try to comfort them. Anything she said right now would sound stupid. Instead, she let them grieve together, and Grey slid back down on the floor once again. She looked at her hands and realized the raw sores on her wrists had begun to heal, thanks to the medicine they'd given her.

The cries of the other prisoners soon quieted down as everyone was probably sitting in cells like this one, contemplating their fate. It didn't make sense. Grey thought she knew why she was here, but why had they imprisoned everyone else?

Soon the Lenoirs composed themselves and turned toward her.

"What happened?" Grey asked.

"They forced us out of the ship and brought us here."

"No explanation?"

Dr. Lenoir shook his head, lowering his voice. "I had noted several anomalies on this flight, you being one of them. Civilian cosmoships normally do not carry prisoners or the head of the Mazdaar High Council."

"You didn't know all those soldiers were on board?"

He sighed, shaking his head again. "Not until we landed."

Grey rested her arms on her knees, staring at the floor. If she had any doubts about them killing her father, she didn't anymore. If he came for her, he would die.

"We've had our suspicions about Mazdaar for many years," Dr. Lenoir whispered.

Grey met the old man's gaze. His shoulders were hunched, his chin a sea of white stubble, but in his eyes something still sparked. She waited for him to explain. He came over to her side of the cell. Tessa did the same until they were sitting on either side of Grey. Tessa still looked shell-shocked, but she was paying attention to her husband.

Grey glanced back and forth between the couple. "Thank you for helping me."

"I can think of no crime to justify why a girl your age should be treated like this."

And Grey noticed that even now he wasn't asking her what she'd done to end up in the clutches of the Mazdaar army.

Tessa reached out and gently touched Grey's battered face. Her lip and nose were still swollen and she hadn't yet been able to clean the dried blood from her face.

"They hurt you again," Tessa said.

"I'm bait for my parents." Grey was ill with the realization. "That's why I'm here. They want Tanner and Sue Alexander, and I have no idea why."

Dr. Lenoir abruptly turned toward her. "You're Tanner and Sue's daughter?"

She hesitated. "Why, do you know them?"

"I worked with your father," he said. "A long time ago."

"How did—"

"It's best you don't know about that," Dr. Lenoir said, lowering his voice. "General Yurkutz can do far worse than macro-shocks."

"But—"

"Trust me, Grey."

She didn't exactly have a choice.

23

After *Tevah* stabilized into a steady flight pattern, Dana helped Rin to the lavatory where she tried to clean her flight suit and get rid of the awful taste in her mouth with a few gulps of water.

"Easy." Dana waved the tap off.

Rin steadied herself against the sink. "Doesn't it bother you at all?"

Crossing her arms, Dana just smiled. "Welcome to space travel."

"Right. I forgot. You probably learned to walk in one of these."

She reached around Dana to wipe her hands on the towel attached to the wall. Everything was smaller and more cramped on the cosmoship.

Luckily, the lavatory had airtight seals to keep sewage where it belonged when pilots took their passengers on stomach-roiling rides into the heavens.

"We'll be there before you know it," Dana said. "You might want to rest up."

She shook her head. How could she have been living with a cosmoship in her home for this long and not realize it could fly her to another planet?

Dana didn't seem bothered by the motion of the floor as the ship flew at speeds Rin couldn't even fathom. In a way, Dana reminded Rin of Grey. They both had the determination and confidence Rin wished she had, but something in Dana's eyes betrayed an inner turmoil Rin had never seen in her sister. She could only imagine what it must feel like for Dana to know her own mother wanted her dead.

"Do we have any idea where Grey is on Jupiter?"

"Orion settlement lies in the very center of the Eye, but until we get under the cloud cover we won't be able to get any visuals."

"Are there really Mazdaar settlements?"

"You sure don't know much, do you?"

Rin swallowed hard. Her stomach was settling, but her emotions were not. Grey was out there on that foreign planet, and she had to find a way to help her when they got there. Mazdaar could be torturing her again at this very moment.

"They started bringing the convicts first," Dana went on, and Rin focused on her. "It was a way to test the Jupiter environment. Not much was known about it forty years ago, and the Mazdaar army wasn't going to volunteer their troops for a death mission on a planet they weren't sure was habitable."

It sounded like a logical Mazdaar plan.

"They were the test subjects," Dana continued. "Since they were all connected, it was easy enough for Mazdaar to track them from orbit and observe whether they survived and how they did it."

"How many lived?"

"More than you'd think." Dana fingered her braid. "But they banded together and declared themselves sovereign. They figured out they were being tracked and cut out their chips. Mazdaar doesn't know exactly where they are on Jupiter anymore. It's a huge planet, and there are lots of places to hide. They don't know where your father is either, and that's why they need Grey."

Rin walked back to the bridge, leaning on the walls as she went. She returned to her seat to find that Mrs. March had turned off the viewing windows and was flying the ship by instruments.

"Won't they see us approach when we enter the atmosphere?" Rin asked.

Mrs. March turned and gave her a smile. "That's what the shields are for."

Leaning back into her seat, she wondered if Grey was now another one of Mazdaar's guinea pigs.

Grey awoke with a start.

Dr. Lenoir knelt beside her and held a finger to his lips. "Shhh . . ."

His shadowy face stared down into hers, and Grey slowly sat up. She must've fallen asleep. Faint light slipped through the slit in the door, creating a huge yellow line on the floor.

"Listen carefully," Dr. Lenoir whispered. "We have ten hours of daylight here. And while there is some oxygen, it is strongest around the trees. The further from them you travel, the harder it will be to breathe. There are other people out there. You'll need to find them, and then you will have a chance."

"What are you talking about?"

Dr. Lenoir knelt inches from her, but she could barely see

his face. Fabric rustled, and she felt him press something metallic into her hand. "This is a skelette. It will unlock the cell door and most other locks in this building too."

She remembered the strange instrument he'd used to undo her restraints. This felt about that size.

"You're young, strong." Dr. Lenoir curled her fingers around the skelette. "You can survive out there."

Grey slowly realized what he was saying. "But what about the two of you?"

"We would only slow you down."

"They'll kill you for helping me."

"Grey." Dr. Lenoir's voice became firm as he stood up. "We have hope. Even if we die, we will be at peace. Can you say as much?"

"I . . . I can't leave you here."

"You must. But there's not much time. They will be changing the guard soon."

She climbed to her feet and began to protest again, but he continued, explaining how the skelette worked. Something about exciting the atoms within the metal chamber of a lock.

"Head for the trees. If you can make it to the forest, you'll be able to hide when the winds come. It will be to your advantage."

"Winds?"

"They come several times each day, and the soldiers are nervous about going off base because of them. Many of their comrades have been killed by the animals."

"What—"

"Meganeura, epicyon, entelodon . . . the winds invigorate them."

Great. If she wasn't killed by Mazdaar, she'd be eaten by unknown wild animals whose names she couldn't even pronounce. How could she get past the guards? And what would happen to this sweet, old couple? Grey thought of how they'd treated her and how their kindness had comforted her. She'd seen firsthand what Mazdaar could do to objectors, and she knew what would happen when they opened this cell and found her missing.

Grey made up her mind. She handed the device back to Dr. Lenoir. "I'm not going without you."

"It's the only way."

"No." She stepped closer to him until she could smell his faint aftershave. "I will not leave you here."

24

Grey stood her ground. She could never live with herself if she abandoned the Lenoirs.

Dr. Lenoir and Tessa seemed to be communicating with each other just through eye contact.

"All right," Dr. Lenoir said. "We will come with you."

"But we must hurry," Tessa added.

Grey held her breath as Dr. Lenoir worked on the lock. His fingers trembled. They'd have only seconds to make their escape as the guards changed shifts.

Holding the skelette directly over the lock, Dr. Lenoir muttered under his breath. When it emitted a faint hum, he grimaced. "Ready?"

Grey could only see a few soldiers, and they had converged in a corner room of the warehouse. Even from here she could hear raucous laughter as they ate their evening meal. This was their chance. The soldiers' backs were turned.

Dr. Lenoir handed Grey the device. "You lead the way.

The moment the cell door opens, we'll slip silently past the other cells and make the run of our lives to that door over there."

Both Grey and Tessa gave Dr. Lenoir quick nods, and he cracked the door open.

"The Lord be with us," Tessa whispered.

Grey hadn't realized how sweltering the cell had been until the cold air of the dome hit them. She could almost see her breath. As one, Grey and the Lenoirs crept along the wall of cells. Could they possibly escape from this armed fortress?

She shook away her fears and focused on placing one silent foot in front of another. The door. Head for the outside door.

Grey could barely breathe, feeling like the soldiers would hear even the minuscule sound. If anyone looked up, they'd be in full view, and she was sure there were cameras. How long before someone sounded the alarm? Would the other prisoners keep quiet?

At the end of the cell row she glanced back to see the soldiers still facing the other way. A few were sitting at tables playing some sort of card game while they ate.

The door to their freedom seemed unguarded. Could the guards have grown lax with them all locked in cells?

Grey tensed, like one of Kildare's cats. The Lenoirs were right behind her.

"Remember what I told you." Dr. Lenoir rested his hand on her shoulder. "Godspeed."

Before she could reply, Dr. Lenoir and Tessa took off running back toward their cell. Away from the door and directly toward the soldiers.

In one horrible second, Grey realized what they were doing. Everything in her wanted to chase after them to divert their suicidal course.

They were creating a diversion. To save her.

"Hey!"

Grey ran.

The scuffing of chairs, the shouting of soldiers and prisoners alike became a blur of noise and gave her enough time to make it to the door. Grey glanced over her shoulder to see a mass of military heading straight toward the Lenoirs.

A whoosh of laser fire sounded. Tessa went down.

Frantic, Grey held the skelette device over the lock, desperately hoping it would work. Had they killed her?

Please, no.

"Stop the girl!"

Shouts rang through the cavernous room. They were coming to get her.

The lock snapped, and Grey flung the door open just as a volley of laser fire shattered the air, hitting the metal wall beside her. Sparks flew into her face, but she ran anyway. The Lenoirs' sacrifice could not be for naught.

Grey flew through the exit and out into the Jupiter air.

She didn't expect it to be dark outside.

Or for a sentry to be stationed right beside the exit.

Without warning, an armored form grabbed her from behind and pinned her arms to her sides.

"I got her!" It was a female voice.

Her fingers still curled around the skelette, Grey fought against her assailant with every instinct she had, jamming her elbows up into the soldier's gut. The sentry wasn't much bigger than she, and Grey took advantage of it.

She kicked back as hard as she could with her foot, hoping to knock out a vulnerable knee. She knew she'd hit her mark when the guard groaned. She wasn't a drone. Drones couldn't feel pain. The sentry's grip loosened, and Grey twisted to escape.

Kicking again, this time she caught only air.

"Out . . . here!" the guard called.

Throwing her head backwards to headbutt the soldier's nose, she slammed instead into the helmet, jarring her own skull. But she couldn't give up.

Grey suddenly made her entire body limp. Her weight slipped out of the guard's grasp, and Grey tumbled to the ground, free again. Rolling, she tried to climb to her feet, but the soldier kicked her in the side. Pain rocketed through her ribs and sucked the air from her lungs.

Grey forced herself to roll farther away. That gave her enough space to get her legs under herself, only to have the guard close the gap again. They faced each other, and in the dim light of the doorway she stared into the woman's eyes, surprised to see they were wide with fear.

The soldier hesitated.

That was all Grey needed. Using both hands to make one big fist, Grey struck the woman in the face as hard as she could. It was enough to send the soldier to the ground, but she righted herself so quickly Grey couldn't get in another hit.

She turned to run again, but the soldier ripped a gun from her holster, leveling it at her chest.

Grey froze. The violetflare handhelds might not blow her in half, but they were deadly. One squeeze of that trigger, and she was gone.

It was over.

But the soldier didn't fire. Instead, she waved the gun at Grey, whispering the one word that saved her life.

"Run."

Grey did, wincing as each stride stabbed her between the ribs. The huge hulk of *Genesis* blocked her path to the right. The weird trees Dr. Lenoir said to head for loomed on the other side of the clearing.

Grey was halfway to them when the rest of the guards burst from the dome. Shots flamed through the night, slicing into the dirt around her, sending up plumes of dust. She'd almost made it without being hit, but then it felt like a blow torch burned her left arm, and she held back a cry. And kept running. She had to survive for Rin!

She imagined the soldiers fanning out behind her. She could hear them yelling into the darkness, their steps matching hers in intensity. The trees. Where were the trees?

Grey stumbled once, catching herself. She almost dropped the skelette but managed to stuff it into her pocket as she ran.

Pitch blackness surrounded her as she blindly ran across the open field farther from the lights of the dome. All she could see now were shadows. At least the soldiers would be having the same problem if they weren't wearing night vision masks.

She nearly jumped out of her skin when a flash of cloud-to-cloud lightning sliced through the sky, illuminating her surroundings. Did that mean the winds were coming? There was no time to be startled by the display. She spotted the trees with their shiny leaves and sprinted toward them.

Another volley of laser fire came from behind her. If one of those beams hit her in the head or torso she wouldn't have a chance.

Grey reached the trees as another flash of thunderless lightning spread through the mass of twisting clouds above her. She stumbled and fell but landed on her hands and knees. A soft, mossy texture met her fingers.

She had no time to ponder the strange flora of Jupiter as she climbed to her feet again and crashed through the grove. The soldiers had to be right behind her, but she didn't hear any more shots.

She flew through the trees with her arms outstretched to protect her face. Branches clawed at her with no mercy. Soon

Grey could run no further and collapsed at the base of one of the trees, its tangled roots breaking her fall. Gasping for air, she shut her eyes and waited for the soldiers to inevitably catch up with her. There was nothing more she could do.

But their shouts grew fainter, even as her pain sharpened. The fight-or-flight rush that had pushed her to safety was quickly fading. Clutching her arm with a trembling hand, Grey felt the warmth of blood soaking into her sleeve and between her fingers. She didn't know how bad the wound was, but for now she was alive.

She thought of the Lenoirs running toward what she hoped was a quick and painless death. Why had they sacrificed their lives for her? Surely, as doctors, they'd seen Mazdaar's cruelty before. She couldn't have been the first patient they'd treated who had suffered at Yurkutz's hand.

Ten-hour days. That meant morning could dawn soon. If she waited here until daylight, Mazdaar would find her for sure.

Another flash of lightning gave her a chance to check her wound. Each heartbeat made her arm throb. She couldn't see how deep it was, but in the stillness of the strange Jupiter forest, she could hear the steady dripping of her blood as it fell to the dried, fallen leaves on the forest floor.

Grey ripped off the end of her sleeve and pressed it as hard as she could on the wound, muffling a gasp at the fiery sting it caused. Hopefully, that would stem some of the bleeding. Hadn't Dr. Lenoir said something about finding other people out here?

With the next lightning flash, she peered through the trees, hoping to see how much distance she'd put between herself and the dome.

Grey gasped.

A figure loomed over her.

25

Grey scrambled, slipping in the leaves, but finally managed to get to her feet. She backed away, clutching her wounded arm.

Run!

She couldn't just stand here and let herself be captured.

A burst of lightning illuminated what was before her—an armored Mazdaar soldier. Grey gathered the little strength she had left and took off again through the woods.

"Wait!" the soldier called.

The female voice sounded familiar.

At the risk of being caught, she slowed and spun around. Grey saw the figure fall to the ground.

"I won't . . . hurt you."

The soldier was now just a mound of dark uniform.

"I . . . let you go," came her faint voice. "Outside the dome."

Squinting, Grey waited for another flash of lightning to

help her see. She needed to get a good look at this woman. Was this a trap?

The guard was wheezing for air.

"Why should I believe you?"

"I told them you headed for *Genesis*."

So that's why the army had stopped their pursuit.

"They shot me because I didn't detain you." The soldier flicked on a small light no larger than a finger and turned it on her own face. The blood from a cut on her temple, probably where Grey had punched her, had dried to a dirty smear.

Still not convinced, Grey cautiously retraced her steps in the direction she'd come, ready to flee at the slightest provocation. The soldier kept the light on her face as Grey closed the distance between them.

"You don't have to help me, but . . ." She grimaced.

Grey dropped to her knees beside her. "Give me the light."

The guard did so without hesitation. Grey yanked the laser off the soldier's belt and stuffed it into her own waistband.

"Why did you let me go?"

"I . . . I don't know."

Shining the light on the woman's body, Grey saw a bloody stain spreading across her side under the graphene breastplate.

"They know where the armor is vulnerable."

Undoing the clasps of the thin mesh plate, Grey helped her slip out of it so she could better examine the wound. Lightning shot across the sky, and Grey quickly scanned the grove. So far, they hadn't been followed, but she was worried about the amount of blood the guard was losing.

"What's your name?"

"Lee."

"Grey."

"It's bad, isn't it?"

She didn't want to answer. If a blueflare caused this wound, it probably would've torn up her insides too.

Lee shifted and tried to sit up against a tree trunk. Using the small torch, Grey glanced at her own arm. A deep gouge carved through her muscle. Using one hand and her teeth, she quickly finished wrapping it with the blood-soaked rag she'd ripped off her shirt.

"They got you too," Lee whispered.

She nodded, wondering how long she could stay here before Mazdaar realized where she'd really headed. She tore off her other sleeve and did her best to bandage Lee's gushing wound.

"They'll keep searching until they find you," Lee said.

Grey tried to guess how far the woods extended and how easily she could navigate through them in the dark. She swiped at her forehead with the back of her good arm. She was pouring sweat from running.

She turned back to Lee. "Can you walk?"

The woman coughed then tried to stand up. Grey shut off the light and stuffed it into her own pocket. This woman wore the Mazdaar star on her uniform. Yet given the chance to kill Grey—something that would've certainly been rewarded—she'd let her go.

Grey wrapped her arm around the woman's shoulders and supported her back. They were about the same height. "Let's go," she said.

Lee took a few steps, struggling, but she didn't complain. The lightning illuminated their path intermittently, enough for them to pick through the trees. Lee tripped but managed to right herself before they both went down. Supporting her was causing Grey's arm to ache, but the exertion kept her from becoming chilled.

"These woods are your only chance," Lee said. "There are places to hide here until dawn."

"What about the winds?"

"They're coming."

"When?"

"Probably soon."

They traveled for almost an hour before Grey couldn't hold Lee up anymore. They both sank to the ground to catch their breath.

At the next flash of light Grey studied the canopy overhead, amazed that the trees seemed to be at least twice as tall as of anything she'd seen on Earth. They twisted and turned upward, never straight for more than a few inches.

"You have to keep moving. Don't let them get you."

They'd rested for less than five minutes when a pungent zing hit Grey's nose like the smell of ozone before a storm in the Preserve, yet sweeter and almost thick. Grey had just enough time to long for home before the winds hit. There was no build up, no warning. Instantly, a rush of warm air hit her, and she cowered down beside Lee, covering her eyes to protect them from the flying dirt, leaves, and bark. The woods roared as the wind crashed through the trees.

Grey wasn't sure how many minutes the blast lasted, but it was an unrelenting, constant gale. Just as suddenly as it began, the winds ceased and the forest became still again.

She started to climb to her feet as a howl pierced the night, so close Grey felt the back of her neck tingle. It sounded like a coyote, yet much larger.

"What was that?"

Even in the darkness, Grey could see the whites of Lee's eyes. "Tasmanian wolves."

26

evah skimmed the surface of Jupiter, and Rin watched the screens with Dana as the crew scanned the ground using infrared to find a suitable landing site. When they located a clearing on the edge of a wood they banked, reversed power, and slowly lowered the ship to the ground.

Touchdown bumped hard. Mrs. March and her crew let out a collective cheer and unstrapped themselves from their seats. Rin joined them in hugs and handshakes. They'd succeeded. They were on Jupiter!

As soon as she could, Rin clambered down into the hold to check on Tram and Trif. She carefully released them from their flight harnesses, making sure they hadn't sustained any injuries. Both were wide-eyed, but they calmed at her touch.

"What'd you think of that, boys?"

Tram whinnied, and Rin wondered if he was missing Grey. Trif had always gravitated to her, but Tram had a special bond with her sister, even if she wasn't always aware of it. Maybe it was because they were both quiet, no-nonsense creatures who'd rather get a job done than fuss about it. She watched the zorses get their footing again in their stalls.

"How are they?"

Rin jumped at Mrs. March's voice. She'd thought the old woman was still on the command deck.

"Okay, I think."

"Good." Mrs. March rested her hand on a stall door. "We're finalizing plans now to send out a scouting team."

Rin stroked Trif on the neck. "She could be anywhere, couldn't she?"

Mrs. March met her gaze with compassion. "Orion settlement is less than twenty kilometers from here. It's our first guess."

"How are we . . ." The reality of how few they were in number was sinking in. Including herself and Dana, they numbered less than thirty. "Do we even have a chance?"

Commander March smiled. "We may be small, dear, but we are prepared. And we're not unarmed." She gestured toward the zorses. "Are you done here?"

Rin nodded.

"Come with me."

She followed Mrs. March out of the hold and into the ship's armory. A long row of blueflare rifles was strapped to one wall, and a vast assortment of gleaming swords and knives lined another. In a closet with clear doors, graphene-armor suits hung ready, and several huge, unmarked crates were stacked in a corner.

"This is not the first time I've been to Jupiter," Mrs. March said.

Rin blinked, trying to take the statement in stride even as her mind whirred.

"I can see this surprises you," Mrs. March said. "Over

forty years ago, I was a Mazdaar military pilot. Once Mars was settled, we started missions to Jupiter about the same time as the Yien Dynasty."

"Dana said they used convicts as test subjects."

"Mazdaar did. And I flew them in." With a sigh, Mrs. March turned toward the wall of weapons. "I was a different person back then. I knew what they were doing to those people, but I still obeyed orders." A muscle in Mrs. March's jaw bunched. "When I found my faith I defected, and I've made it my life's mission to somehow make up for what I did back then."

"So this is personal to you," Rin said.

"From day one. And when they took your parents and now Grey . . ." Mrs. March pulled down one of the rifles. "Just know I want to find them as much as you do."

"It seems hopeless," Rin whispered.

Mrs. March checked the power level of the weapon and returned it to its wall mount. "Even in the darkest night, there is always hope."

The howling echoed through the dark, somewhere way too close.

"Tasmania wolves?" Grey whispered.

Lee nodded. "But not like any you've ever seen before."

An eerie call seemed to answer.

"Some call them thylacine," Lee said softly. "They're extinct on Earth."

"How'd they get *here*?"

"No idea."

Grey felt queasy as another lupine joined in. That made at least three. They were sitting ducks if these wolves were hungry.

"Think you can keep moving?"

When Lee didn't respond, she dared to flick on the light again. Lee's bandage glistened with fresh, crimson blood, and her eyelids drooped.

Grey shook her. "No. Stay awake."

"Please . . ." Lee's eyes opened but looked beyond Grey. "You must leave me. It's okay."

"I won't."

"I'm going to die here." Lee clutched Grey's arm with trembling, sticky fingers. "But you can make it."

Leaning toward her, Grey spoke directly into Lee's ear. "You are not dying on my watch, so quit talking like that."

"I don't deserve to live."

A panicky feeling bubbled up inside her at how faint Lee's voice was sounding.

"I'm sorry for what . . . I've done," Lee said. "But it's too late."

What could she possibly say to this woman? Shivering, Grey knelt beside her. She grabbed Lee's hand. She shouldn't care about a Mazdaar soldier who might have killed or even tortured people, but Grey couldn't leave her to die alone. Lightning flashed. Lee's face was ashen.

Once when she was very young, Mom had sat by her bed while Grey's small body fought a virus not even her mother's strongest herbs could cure. She was barely lucid from fever, but Grey still remembered some of her mother's whispered prayers.

If I go up to the heavens, you are there.

Lifting her gaze to the treetops, Grey felt tears drip from her eyes.

A stick cracked somewhere to their left, and Grey strained toward the sound, yanking out Lee's gun. She'd never shot a laser pistol before, but she would not leave Lee at the mercy of these wild animals.

Grey stood and shined the torch in the direction of the sound, and a pair of eyes glowed, then disappeared. Her heart hammered, intensifying the ache in her arm. If a wolf came any closer she would have to shoot it. But if she did, the shot could alert anyone nearby.

"Please move on," she muttered. "Nothing to see here."

A long, low howl reverberated through the woods, ending in a deep snarl. She pointed her light into the trees, and two more sets of eyes reflected back at her.

Twigs snapped again, this time from her other side. Grey had the horrible feeling they were being surrounded. And the howls were coming from both sides of them now.

"How big are they?"

Lee didn't answer.

Grey dropped to the ground again and tried to help her stand. "We can't just sit here and let them attack us! We have to start moving."

"It doesn't matter."

"It has to." She tried to pull Lee up, but the soldier was a limp weight.

"Lee, come on!"

Musk filled her nose, even as a nearby growl chilled her to the core. Grey let Lee lie back down and clutched the gun, slowly rising to her feet again. Each time she turned on her light she took a risk the soldiers would see them, but Grey had to know how many wolves she was up against. She flicked on the beam, shining it into the woods.

That's when she saw it.

There wasn't even time to shout a warning to Lee before the animal darted directly in front of her, teeth bared. A fierce rumble billowed from its throat.

He crouched, his thick, striped tail wagging nervously, the hackles along his back spiked in formation. The Tasmanian wolf's face looked like a cross between a cougar and a dog, but his jaw opened twice as wide.

Grey raised the gun as two more angry lupines emerged from the shadows. She swung toward them, gauging the distance.

Three! How could she shoot three? Spinning back to the first, she aimed for the spot between his eyes right as the third wolf lunged at her.

She fired.

The laser beam sizzled through the air, but the wolf had dodged out of the way at the last moment. Instantly upon her, the wolf behind her latched onto her wounded arm, knocking her to the ground. Landing hard on her right shoulder, the gun flew from her grasp.

The animal shook her with its massive jaws and Grey shrieked in agony, desperately pounding its head with her other fist.

It was like hitting a furry rock.

Lee was right. They were both as good as dead. She'd never see Rin again.

Just when she felt like she was going to pass out, harsh voices broke through the forest. A light temporarily blinded her. A flurry of men rushed into the clearing, shouting and warding off the Tasmanian wolves with clubs, boots, and curses. The wolf let go of her, yelping off into the woods with the others.

Grey curled into a ball, whimpering. The razor-sharp teeth had ripped deep into her wound.

"Terminate them," a deep voice said.

"But we have orders."

"To Hades with orders."

"They're wounded anyway."

"Shut up, both of you! Have you no decency?"

Grey cracked open her eyes. A bearded man with wire-rimmed glasses stood over her and two other men surrounded Lee, who wasn't moving. One of them held a lantern of some kind; another picked up the gun Grey had dropped.

The bearded man knelt in front of Grey. He reached for her wounded arm, but she recoiled, pulling it closer to her chest. Please. No more pain.

"Let me see," he said.

"She's worse," Grey managed. "Shot. In the side. Help her. I'm only grazed."

The man waved a hand to a rangy guy with long hair. "Get over here, Rusty. Shine your light."

Another lantern was held in front of Grey's face, and she squinted. Who were these men?

"Bring the other one over here."

By the light of the lanterns, which contained some sort of fiery liquid inside a clear cylinder, Grey could make out her arm. The wolf had torn away most of her makeshift bandage, and the wound was pouring blood again, fresh slices carved into the original gash that had taken a chunk from her triceps. She clamped down on it with her right hand. She would refuse any help until these men did what they could for Lee, who appeared half-dead already.

Two of them carried Lee over and laid her down next to Grey. Her eyes were closed now. The man with the glasses dug in a pack and produced a clean towel and a canteen. A knife with a blade as long as his forearm came from his belt. Without words, he removed Lee's blood-soaked bandage and cut at her shirt to further expose her wound.

"What kind of weapon was it?" he asked.

"Blueflare, I think."

He pressed the towel into the open wound. Lee didn't make a sound.

Grey tried to sit up, but the forest pirouetted around her in a wave of nausea. She took in a deep breath, trying to focus. What if the soldiers saw these lights and came after them all?

"Who are you?" she asked in a whisper.

"The more important question is who are you?"

Grey focused on breathing, and the excruciating fire seemed to loosen some of its grip. She glanced at each scruffy man. They were all dressed in rugged, mismatched clothing, and she noted their muscular bulk. She didn't have a chance if they intended her harm. She'd escaped the soldiers, but what if this group was worse? At least the soldiers had left her alone in her cell.

The guy holding Lee's laser gun approached, glaring down at the soldier. "She's Mazdaar," he practically spat.

"I am well aware of that." The man with the glasses—she noticed one of the lenses was cracked—wiped Lee's blood off his hands into another rag. Then to Grey he said, "I'm Pierce."

Kneeling in front of Grey once more, he reached for her wound. This time, Grey let him touch her. Adrenaline still surged through her veins, and she quivered with fear as much as with pain. She closed her eyes as he wrapped her wound like he had Lee's side.

"You aren't Mazdaar," Pierce said.

She opened her eyes. "What are you going to do to us?"

He offered her the canteen. "To dull the pain," he said.

She sniffed at it, realizing it was some sort of liquor. Grey took a long swallow and grimaced as it bit the back of her throat.

"Now let's try this again," Pierce said. "Start with your name."

With effort, Grey tried to get up, and Pierce took hold of her hand to help. The forest spun again but gradually settled. She remembered how Dr. Lenoir had said there were others out here.

You'll need to find them, and then you'll have a chance.

"Grey," she said.

Pierce jerked a thumb at Lee. "Her?"

The lanterns brightened the clearing enough that Grey got her first good look at the Mazdaar soldier who had saved her life. She might've been about thirty with short, dark hair and olive skin.

"Her name is Lee."

Finley kicked at the stripes on her sleeve with the toe of his boot. "A sergeant."

"Why are you with a Mazdaar soldier?"

"I was a prisoner. She helped me escape, and they shot her for it."

Pierce raised an eyebrow.

"They're probably still looking for me."

"Can you walk?"

She nodded.

"Then we better get moving."

"Where are we going?"

Pierce eyed her with annoyance. He turned toward the others. "Grab some branches, men. We'll need to carry the soldier."

Two of them obeyed, but the man who'd looked at Lee like he wanted to finish her off right there crossed his arms, staring down Pierce.

"I'm not rescuing a Mazdaar soldier," he said.

27

Pierce held his ground. "You will if I say so, Finley."

"What if she's connected?"

"We can remove her implant," Pierce said, waving toward Lee, who was still unconscious.

"She saved my life," Grey said.

Finley jabbed a finger in her face. "And who's *she*? You're just gonna believe what she says?"

Grey started to protest, "I—"

Pierce silenced her with an upraised hand. He leaned toward Finley, his voice low. "I'm making this call. Is that understood?"

When Finley failed to respond, Pierce grabbed him by the shirt. "Is it?"

The other man twisted out of Pierce's grasp, muttering. But he backed down.

The men quickly made a stretcher for Lee using large branches and vines. Finley and the long-haired man carried her, while Grey walked behind Pierce, cradling her elbow.

"Do the winds really make the animals hunt?" she asked in a whisper.

"Who told you that?"

Grey hesitated. "A friend."

"Yes," he said. "You might have been their dinner tonight."

They were traveling without using their lights now that dawn glowed through the swirling clouds. But Grey still had to focus to keep from tripping on a root or slamming into Pierce when he stopped suddenly to listen. Once she thought she spotted a lupine deep in the trees, but it quickly bounded away when it saw them.

"Are those Tasmanian wolves from Earth?" she asked.

"You ask too many questions."

Grey shut up at the rebuke and concentrated on her footing. They hadn't bound her, but she still felt like a prisoner. She wondered if Lee would live through the night.

"They were here when we arrived," Pierce finally said. "They're only vicious when the winds come. Drives them mad or something. Be glad an entelodon didn't find you. Your arm would be gone."

She didn't dare ask him how he'd ended up on the planet himself. Mrs. March had mentioned convicts. Was he one of them? If so, she might have just as much to fear from these men as she did from Mazdaar.

When they reached the edge of the woods, Grey gaped at the landscape. Before them was not the cold, utilitarian dome from which she'd escaped, but a vast stretch of plateaus and mesa-like mountains, so similar to home that she felt a pang in her chest. It was a comforting sight, until she looked up at the tumultuous sky, now brilliant with oranges and purples. Even during the worst summer storm, she'd never seen anything like it on Earth.

"We can rest here," Pierce said, pausing to allow the men to lay the stretcher down for a moment.

"Thank you for helping us." Grey said as she turned back to Lee's stretcher. The soldier's eyes were open now, though her face was still as pale as cirrus clouds.

"She's awake, sir."

Pierce stared down at Lee, his presence commanding yet not as threatening as Finley's. "How many soldiers are stationed at Orion?"

Lee clutched at her side struggling for a breath. She glanced between the men who peered down at her menacingly. "Five squadrons," she finally said, "and eighty-two prisoners."

"What is the mission?"

"I was told we were to provide security for a new settlement."

Finley swore. "What did I tell you?"

"Can they track you?"

Lee hesitated. "On Earth, yes. I don't know about here."

Grey hadn't thought of that. Lee's Dot implant could betray them all if Mazdaar had that technology in place up here. And why wouldn't they?

Pierce focused on his men. "They'd need satellites in orbit for long-distance range, which they don't have yet. But the further we get from Orion the better."

He started walking again, leading them down a rockstrewn slope toward the buttes in the distance. Grey marveled at how Jupiter sometimes mimicked Earth, like when they passed a red-rocked butte that could've fit well in the dry, arid Alamo Republic.

Then she'd see a field of lush, green grass as fine as hair stretching up along the sides of the butte. Could there be an underground spring feeding the vegetation? It was flourishing where no grass would have a chance back home.

"What will you do with us?" Grey finally gathered up the nerve to ask.

A grumble came from behind her, probably Finley.

"That'll be up to the captain to decide," Pierce said.

As they traveled on, Grey felt as if she'd drop from exhaustion, or was it the thin air? She stumbled over a rock and would've landed on her knees if Pierce hadn't caught her.

"Just a little further," he said. "Can you make it?"

She stared up into his rugged face, unable to read his expression through his brown beard and glasses. "Yeah."

They treaded up an incline as they neared several huge buttes, and the ground turned sandy. Her vision was starting to blur as Pierce led their party straight toward one of the massive rocks. He stepped right up to it, and Grey squinted to see any kind of opening. He waved his hand across its surface, and the entire face of the rock shimmered and became like fabric. She'd never seen such a large piece of chameleon cloth. Pulling the fabric away, Pierce revealed an actual wooden door wide enough for three men to walk through shoulder-to-shoulder.

Had she escaped from one prison only to enter another? If Grey had had any strength left, she would've run. But even if she mustered the will to fight, she was surrounded. Pierce alone could probably pummel her without breaking a sweat.

They led her forward, and Grey cast a frantic glance back at Lee who'd passed out again. Would they kill her?

Pierce took hold of Grey's good arm. Grey panicked and jerked away from him. She was stranded on a planet with convicts and vicious, extinct creatures. She'd almost died only a few hours ago. Her father was somewhere out there being manipulated by Yurkutz, and she might never see her little sister again.

"Hey," Pierce said. "Relax. We're not going to hurt you."

But what if he was lying? What really awaited her if she stepped into this cave? She backed up, but Pierce blocked her way. Grey was pulling in jerky breaths, partially from the low oxygen, but mostly from the horrible realization she might've walked right into a deadly trap.

Pierce tried to forcibly push her into the cave right as the door swung open and three people, two men and a woman, stepped out. The men looked like they were cut from the same cloth as Pierce and his companions, with unshaven faces and grubby clothes. The woman's cargo pants and scuffed boots fit right in too.

"Captain," Pierce said.

Grey took advantage of his diverted attention and tried to yank away from him again, but his fingers now closed around her wounded arm too. She almost doubled over.

"What in the world is going on?"

The woman stepped forward, and Grey gave up. It was futile. She wasn't going anywhere.

"We found these two in the woods. Both wounded."

That's when Grey saw the face of the woman they called Captain, and their eyes met. Neither of them moved.

"Grey?"

A jolt shot through her bones when she heard the captain's voice. "Mom?"

28

Ever since General Yurkutz ignited the spark of hope that her parents might still be alive, Grey hadn't allowed herself to fully believe it was true. Even when she saw Dad on the screen, she had doubt. It could still have been one big Mazdaar lie fabricated to coerce her into sharing the secrets they thought she had. But as Grey tried to take a step toward the woman who looked and sounded so much like her mother, her hope came to life.

"Is it really you?" Grey's legs buckled.

The captain rushed over. "Oh, dear Lord!"

Before Grey collapsed, she was enclosed in the embrace she missed so much. Every time she climbed the ridge and watched the sunset, every day she stood in the silo's galley trying to remember how to cook something, every time Rin asked her to tell another story about Mom or Dad, Grey had yearned for that hug again. She never told Rin how hard it was to fill Mom's shoes. She didn't even admit it to herself sometimes. But in that moment, when Sue Alexander held her for the first time in five years, all the loneliness and grief overcame Grey, and she sobbed against her mother's shoulder.

"My Grey. My little Grey."

She felt real, sounded real. This was no deceptive hologram. Her mother was alive.

They held each other until Pierce finally cleared his throat.

"Captain, I don't understand."

Mom released her, shamelessly wiping away a river of tears that had snaked down her tan cheeks. "This is my daughter." She gently touched the bloodied bandage on her arm. "Where did you find her?"

"The woods," Pierce answered. "Right after the winds, just as the wolves were closing in." He pointed at Grey. "But not before one attacked her. The other's a Mazdaar soldier, as you can see, and this one said she was an escaped prisoner from Orion settlement. There are five new army squadrons and eighty-two more prisoners."

"A prisoner?" Her mother searched her face, but Grey wasn't sure this was the right time to explain. She had too many questions herself.

Mom took one look at Lee and quickly gestured toward the cave entrance. "Take her to the infirmary. Scan her. Remove and destroy her Dot immediately. Finley, stay with her. We'll question her later." She eyed Grey's bandage again. "And tell Sharaya I'll need her to treat my daughter."

Grey watched her mom, still barely comprehending what was happening. The last time they'd been together, Mom had been a foot taller than she; now they stood eye-to-eye. Mom's hair was longer and pulled off her face in a low knot. The khaki cargo pants and white tunic with holes in the sleeves were almost exactly like those Grey had seen in Yurkutz's hologram.

Could she possibly be hallucinating? Had she passed out somewhere in the forest and become delirious?

"Is this really happening?" Grey whispered.

Mom wrapped her arm around Grey and helped her through the large doorway. "I think so, honey. Can you walk okay?"

She nodded, but at the threshold she stumbled. Her mother quickly steadied her and guided her into the cave.

Inside, Grey couldn't see a thing. It was as if day had turned to night with the snap of her fingers. She kept walking, and with each step her eyes adjusted.

They traveled down a passage that emptied into an enormous gallery, lit by more lanterns like those Pierce and the men had in the woods. She felt like she might pass out again, tripping when they took a turn into another tunnel off the main space.

Her mother's arm tightened around her. "Almost there, sweetheart."

"How long . . . have you been here?"

"Five very long years."

When they came to a small cavern off the tunnel, Mom let her go long enough to light two more lanterns inside. Several paper maps hung from the stone walls near a small, folding table. Was this her mother's office?

A rustic cot was made up, and Mom eased her onto it, brushing the back of her fingers against Grey's cheek. For a moment, Grey thought she felt her mother's hand tremble.

Grey allowed herself to lie back onto the thin mattress. "I thought you were dead."

"I know."

"You're going to explain all this, I hope."

"I'll try, but . . . is Rin okay?"

Grey nodded. "She's at home. Safe."

A petite woman with long, salt-and-pepper hair entered carrying a metal case in her arms.

"This is medic Sharaya," Mom said.

The woman scooted a stool up to Grey's cot and started to peel away the makeshift bandage on her arm while her mother held one of the lanterns close to illuminate the wound. "Laser?" Sharaya asked.

"I think."

"Did it bleed a lot, honey?"

"Yeah. The wolf ripped it deeper though." She clenched her teeth at the sting of air on the open wound. "Mom, how did those animals get here?"

"They've been here as long as we have," her mother answered. "Extinct on Earth but thriving on Jupiter."

Grey bit her lip trying to suppress a whimper. She almost wished she could pass out as Sharaya cleaned the deep gash. By the time the medic finished debriding the wound and was carefully bandaging it with fresh gauze, Grey could feel sweat dripping down her face.

"You're a trooper," Sharaya said, then addressed her mother. "It's not life threatening. Keep it clean, watch for infection, and have the bandage changed twice a day." She gave a wistful sigh. "If only I still had my light machine, I could heal it up right now."

Then Sharaya walked out, her cheerful humming echoing off the walls. Grey closed her eyes and tried to focus on anything but her throbbing arm.

Mom knelt beside the cot, holding her hand. "I'm so sorry," she whispered.

"Where's Dad?"

Her mother frowned. "I don't know."

29

Mrs. March put Rin and half a dozen others to work unloading crates and setting up makeshift quarters for the animals outside *Tevah*, something Rin was more than willing to do. She needed to stay busy. Otherwise, she'd go crazy worrying about Grey.

Rin paused on the ramp, mesmerized. Her first look at the Jupiter surface took her breath away. They'd landed in a world full of colors more brilliant than any she'd seen in the Preserve. The dirt wasn't just brown or red. Distinctive yellows, reds, and blues swirled together like a rainbow.

Mountains that dwarfed the Himalayans she'd seen in one of Mrs. March's books stretched up to the roiling clouds. The entire sky glowed with a deep, orange hue. How could she even be alive standing here?

The first thing Tram and Trif did when she released them in their pen was roll in the rainbow dirt. They got up and shook, specks of color now sparkling on their coats. She smiled, thankful to still have them as friends. She might be needing them in her search for Grey.

Please help me find her.

It was getting easier to send up little prayers, and she wondered if being around people like Mrs. March, who never seemed to lose hope, was why. Or maybe it was just being a million miles from home.

As Rin finished feeding the zorses, one of the Jeeps she'd seen in the hold pulled out of the cosmoship with Dana at the wheel. She waved at Rin.

Waving back, Rin stared at the strange vehicle. She'd seen cars a few times before when she and Grey had ventured deeper into the Alamo Republic, but she'd never ridden in one. Nobody she knew could afford an antique like that in the Preserve, and they would have trouble finding fuel anyway.

Dana swung the Jeep over to her, skidding to a stop and sending a plume of colored dust into the air. "Hop in."

She laughed at how Dana had to yell to be heard over the Jeep's thrumming engine. "Seriously?"

"I've gotta do some scouting. Thought you might like to come along."

Rin was all over it. It would be good to familiarize herself with the lay of the land. It might help her find Grey later. She jumped in, and with a grin, Dana shot the Jeep across the landscape. Jupiter stretched before her, and Rin was in awe of it.

"Pretty amazing, huh?" Dana shouted as they drove around the largest tree Rin had ever seen. Its trunk contorted toward the churning, peach-colored clouds above.

She had no words. Amazing hardly cut it. All she could do was gawk at the weird vegetation.

When she saw some sort of large bird—or was it a giant insect?—shoot in front of the windshield, she grabbed Dana's arm with a gasp.

"What was that?"

Dana didn't slow down as the creature flew by, banked, and dove down at the Jeep again. As it approached, Rin saw it actually had four translucent wings and a yellow body like a bee.

"Probably a type of meganeura," Dana said.

Rin gaped. "You're kidding!"

Dana chuckled, and Rin pressed back into her seat as the engine roared. The Giant Dragonfly? She'd read about them. They'd been extinct on Earth for thousands of years. How did they end up here? Had Mazdaar resurrected them, or were they native to this planet?

She was still pondering the dragonfly twenty minutes later. Dana had yet to stop or even slow.

"What sort of scouting mission is this?"

"An important one."

"For what?"

Dana grimaced. "Secret."

"Then why did you bring me? What are we looking for?"

"Don't worry."

"I'd like to help if I could." How far could they have traveled from *Tevah* by now? Rin twisted around in her seat but couldn't see the ship anymore. "Shouldn't we be in contact with the others? Did you tell them where we were going?"

Dana looked at her like she was a child and pulled the Jeep over beside a bunch of the purple scrubs. "No."

"Why not?"

"They trust me. It wasn't necessary."

"But—"

"Just shut up."

Rin eyed the older girl. Her hands were wrapped around the Jeep's steering wheel with a white-knuckled grip.

"What's your problem?" Rin asked.

"This wasn't how I wanted it to go, okay?"

"I'm sure none of this is easy for you," Rin said, "but it isn't for me either."

Dana closed her eyes. "I'm sorry, Rin."

She searched Dana's face. Had she brought her all the way out here to tell her bad news? "Oh, please, no. Grey isn't—"

"It's not Grey." Dana reached into her coat.

Rin watched in horror as she pulled out a stun pistol. "What are you—"

Dana quickly pressed it to Rin's neck and pulled the trigger.

Everything went black.

Mom stared into Grey's eyes. "Your father and I were on a Yien mission to rescue as many of the prisoners on this planet as we could. But when we hit the lower levels of the atmosphere, something went wrong—I now think it was the winds, but we didn't know about them at the time I made the call as the captain to abandon the ship, and your father obeyed my order. He ejected with the rest of the crew."

Mom squeezed Grey's hand. "I stayed on the bridge until the last moment, hoping I'd find some way to stabilize the ship, but when there was no hope, I ejected too. We searched for weeks, but we never found him."

Grey was shaking her head. "But I saw him. I saw Dad." She held out her wrists, showing her mother the raw marks from the shock cuffs. "General Yurkutz was using me to find both of you. She was communicating with him somehow. I—"

"You *saw* your father?"

"I didn't know if it was real, but yeah, I saw an image of him. Yurkutz was talking to him on some sort of screen. She told him he knew what she wanted and that he had three days to bring it to Orion settlement or else she'd hurt me even more."

Mom pressed her fingers to her mouth. "I hoped . . . oh, Grey, I hoped so much, but . . . are you sure it was him?"

"He had a beard, but it was him."

"Oh, thank you, Lord." Mom gave her another hug.

"Why does Mazdaar want Dad?" Grey asked.

"How much has Mrs. March told you?"

"I didn't even know Jupiter was habitable until a few days ago."

She listened intently to her mother's story, and Grey began to realize she could never see her mother the same way again. She was a pilot, Dad a brilliant scientist. And the cosmoship in their silo was part of it all.

"They want your father for his brains," Mom said. "He's been on the run from them ever since he was your age."

Her mother knelt down beside the cot. "I can't tell you how much I hated leaving you." Mom swallowed, glancing away.

"It's okay."

Mom shook her head. "No it's . . . not. It's not."

She held her mother's hand, understanding traveling between them. They'd lost five years.

"I thought about you and Rin every single day."

"Mrs. March helped us."

Her mother smiled. "I knew she would."

"Where did you get all this stuff?" Grey gestured toward the maps, tables, and equipment in the gallery.

"Most if it was scavenged from the remains of a crashed Mazdaar cosmoship."

"How have you managed to stay hidden? Their settlement's so close." Grey pictured the dome and the soldiers. Even after running most of the night and the journey with Pierce and his men, she'd probably only traveled twenty kilometers, if that.

Mom gave a wave in the direction of the settlement. "It's different on Jupiter. Mazdaar's technology is very limited here, at least for now. Even a lot of the equipment we salvaged is obsolete. The Lord had a plan in all this, I think. We've been able to learn a lot about Jupiter in the hopes that somehow Commander March and the others will be able to join us before Earth is completely taken over."

Grey looked away, not wanting to openly disagree with her mother about the God stuff. It was hard to understand how God could've planned for them to spend five years thinking they were orphans.

"Dad's playing right into their hands. He's going to do what they want."

Sue Alexander rested her hand on Grey's leg, then stood and walked over to the table in the middle of the room where Grey noticed some sort of black weapon sitting out in the open. Mom ignored the gun and brought over a map. Jet would've paid a fortune for something like that on Earth. Hand drawn, it included detailed topography of the area around the camp and outward toward the range named the Castle Mountains.

"But how did they even contact Dad? Is there any way to figure out where he is? We could warn him."

"We've exhausted every attempt to find him."

Just then Pierce stuck his head in the doorway. "Captain?" He jerked a thumb toward the cavern. "We need you. Now."

30

W hat's the problem?" Mom asked, not leaving Grey's side. "Because if it can wait, my daughter and I are—"

"The soldier you sent to the infirmary, she—"

Grey struggled to sit up, feeling woozy.

"Yes?" Mom asked.

"Actually," Pierce nodded at Grey, "she's asking for your daughter."

Mom turned to Grey. "What happened to you, sweetheart? How do you know this soldier?"

"She helped me escape." Grey quickly explained, noting how her mother blanched when she spoke of getting shot.

"Captain, if you're going to question her, you'll want to hurry. They don't expect her to make it."

Grey had known Lee's wound was bad, but she'd still hoped the people here could do something for her. She climbed to her feet without help, ready to go wherever Pierce led them.

At the infirmary, which was another cavity off the main cavern, Pierce held open the cloth door for them. Grey was surprised at how bright the lanterns made everything. She spotted medic Sharaya along with Finley and an armed female guard.

Three cots made out of logs lashed together were lined up against the wall. Only one was occupied, and Grey rushed to it. Lee was lying very still, her eyes closed. Grey feared the worst but then saw the sergeant's chest rise and fall. The smell of pungent antiseptic surrounded the bed.

"I'm surprised she's made it this long," Sharaya whispered to Mom.

Grey leaned over the cot. The woman's eyes fluttered open. When she saw Grey, she tried to speak. "I . . ." Lee swallowed. "I'm glad . . . you got away."

"Thanks to you."

Lee gave her a weak smile, and Grey felt herself choking up. Would she disappoint her mother by caring about this soldier?

Mom came over. "I'm sorry, soldier, but I need to ask you some questions."

Giving a nod, Lee shifted in the cot.

"My name is Captain Sue Alexander, and I appreciate you helping Grey more than you can know."

Lee coughed. "She is a . . . brave girl."

"I know."

"Mazdaar . . . we . . . we aren't all evil," Lee whispered.

"We need to know about your mission here."

Lee closed her eyes, her breath rattling in her throat.

Finley stood beside Mom. "We can get the information out of her."

"No."

"But, Captain—"

"I said no." Mom stepped right up to Finley, invading his personal space. "We will not stoop to their level."

Opening her eyes again, Lee stared up at Mom. Did she have a mother back on Earth who would grieve?

"Don't let them . . . get my body." Lee's voice was barely audible. "Please."

Her mother nodded.

"The prisoners." Lee coughed again, and a dribble of crimson appeared on her lips. "They're going to use them to make . . . drones."

Mom leaned closer. "What?"

Lee's eyes half closed and a gurgling came from her chest. Finley spun on his heels and marched out.

"Lee, please," Grey whispered, begging the woman to hang onto life yet knowing it was too late. Lee had realized she was going to die right from the beginning, hadn't she?

As the dying Mazdaar warrior's chest stopped rising, Grey sidled close to her mother.

All was quiet. They stared down at the utter stillness of Lee's body.

"What did she mean?" Grey said as Mom gently led her out of the room.

Captain Sue Alexander straightened her shoulders, the muscles in her neck tensing into cords. "They're going to execute the prisoners and use their bodies to make drones."

31

As Rin regained consciousness, she realized her hands and legs were bound. A gag that smelled like oil was stuffed in her mouth, and she was lying on something hard and metallic. A scratchy blindfold squeezed around her head, its knot digging into the back of her skull. She thrashed her body in all directions trying to loosen her bonds but only ended up making everything tighter.

An engine roared, and the floor beneath her vibrated. She continued to struggle against her restraints, even though it wasn't helping. She guessed she was lying in the back of the Jeep. Where was Dana taking her? How long would it be before Mrs. March realized something was wrong?

The truth was dawning. Dana must be an infiltrate, and Mrs. March and the entire crew could be in as much danger as she was.

Rin wanted to scream through her gag. Mom and Dad had risked their lives for this girl helping her defect from Mazdaar.

Had everything Dana said to her been a lie?

She listened. Hard.

The Jeep's engine rumbled steadily, and her cheeks dug into the cold, grooved metal.

Please help me.

She lost track of time. Her hands went numb. Her back ached. When they finally stopped, Rin was ready to fight. A well-aimed kick might buy her a few seconds, but what then? She couldn't exactly run away all tied up like this.

Rin thought she heard Dana muttering from the driver's seat.

Someone shouted, and the Jeep's door squeaked open.

"I'm unarmed," Dana said.

Liar.

A male voice spoke back, but Rin couldn't understand the words. Her pulse throbbed in her ears. If Dana had taken her to Orion settlement, Grey could be here too! Maybe this was how she would find her.

Suddenly, the back door of the Jeep flung open, and rough, gloved hands dragged her out and flung her to the ground. Someone ripped the blindfold off, and she blinked at the Mazdaar MP scowling down at her.

All thoughts of fighting vanished as she stared down the barrel of his violetflare gun. Dana stood beside him, another Mazdaar soldier training a laser on her too. Wasn't Dana on *their* side? Then Rin remembered how she said her mother had put a price on her head. Would these guards try to collect?

"I told you," Dana said. "Take me to my mother."

The sentry laughed a deep, who-the-heck-do-you-think-you-are laugh. "I'm sure she'll be thrilled to see you."

His partner chuckled back.

Rin tried to catch Dana's eye, but she wouldn't meet her gaze.

"And who's *she?*" The taller soldier ripped the gag from Rin's mouth, and she gulped in fresh air. Grit coated her teeth. She spit some of it out.

"Tanner and Sue Alexander's youngest daughter," Dana said.

Exchanging looks, the soldiers seemed to silently confer.

Rin surreptitiously took in as much as she could of her surroundings. A huge, black cosmoship, probably ten times larger than *Tevah*, hulked beside a domed building. Beyond, a thick grove of weird trees stood like sentries. She licked at her cracked lips.

"This'll be interesting," the guard muttered, jerking his head toward the dome. He aimed his gun at Rin's ankles and shot at the ropes. They disintegrated in a burst of flame, and she yelped.

The soldier rolled his eyes. "Oh, relax. It was low voltage. Now get up and move."

Wincing at the sting and trying not to glance down at her scorched pants, Rin stumbled to her feet and nearly fell, her thighs and calves tingling from lack of circulation. And she was sure that beam had eaten through more than rope.

The taller soldier poked Dana in the back. "Both of you."

Dana glowered at him but finally complied, falling into step beside Rin. The guards trailed them, weapons drawn and ready. Rin's shoulder brushed against Dana's arm.

"Why'd you do this?" she whispered.

The only response was the crunching of boots in the rainbow-colored dirt.

With Lee's revelation still ringing in her ears, Grey mechanically followed her mother out of the infirmary down another passageway in the rock which wove through the massive cave this group apparently called home.

"I thought drones were man-made robots."

"They used to be," Mom said.

Grey remembered the drones she'd seen in Mazdaar City. Their skin had looked and felt so real. Was that because it *was?*

"How long have they—"

"Years." Mom kept up a fast pace, leading the way. "They first experimented with body parts, but they found limitations working with bodies that had been dead for more than a few minutes. After eight minutes brain cells die. Mazdaar has been trying to make a drone from an intact human body since before you were born."

Using body parts from casualties was one thing. But could they really have brought those people to Jupiter to harvest their flesh?

"Grey." Mom stopped and rested her hand on her daughter's shoulder. "Before I knew him, your father invented a special chip that mimics the electronic signals of the human brain, something that would allow Mazdaar to do this. When he found out what his invention would be used for, he destroyed it. Mazdaar wasn't exactly happy with him."

"That's why they want him now, isn't it? To make those chips."

"And it's just like Evangeline to use his own children as collateral."

"But I escaped."

"Your father probably doesn't know that, and Evangeline certainly isn't going to tell him."

Mom started walking again. Her expression was grim yet determined. She waved over the female guard who'd been following them. "Tell Pierce to gather everyone. Twenty minutes."

Back in what seemed to be her mother's quarters, Mom guided Grey over to the cot again. "I want you to rest."

"But—"

"Please, Grey."

She sat on the bed, a million questions coming to her lips. A part of her wanted to let her mother take care of her, but for five years Grey had been the one in charge. Did her mother have any idea what that had been like, to be twelve and have to make the decisions of an adult? She'd rocked a crying eight-year-old Rin to sleep for weeks.

"Why couldn't you have told us you were working for the Yien Dynasty and Mrs. March?"

Kneeling down in front of her, Mom held Grey's hands in her own. "I would trust you with my life, but I would not trust Mazdaar with yours." She turned Grey's hands up to reveal the worst of the burn scars on her wrists. "Look what they did to you. I couldn't knowingly put you and your sister at risk. That's why we couldn't tell you anything. I hated lying to you, sweetheart. I hope you'll forgive me for that."

That's when Grey noticed that her mother had scars on her wrists too. Had they always been there?

"I know what they're capable of," Mom whispered. "Your father and I wanted to spare you, but apparently we didn't succeed."

"I wish I'd known who you guys really were." Wouldn't things have been different if she had? She might've trusted Jet more or asked Mrs. March more questions.

"Honey, you were just a girl. We were planning to tell you and Rin everything when you got older."

Grey sighed, rubbing her eyes. She wanted to rejoice at this reunion with her mother, but how could she when Rin was practically a galaxy away and she still had no idea where her father was?

Grey noticed strands of white weaving through Mom's hair that hadn't been there years ago. Being separated from her children had to have been terrible for her. She probably felt responsible for Dad too.

"I never gave up hope that I'd see you again." Mom smiled, reaching out to touch her cheek, almost as if she was making sure Grey was real.

"Rin always believed you'd come back."

Mom blinked quickly. "Oh, little Rin."

"She's almost as tall as me, but she's still thin as a twig." Grey fingered her bandage to keep from looking into Mom's eyes. "She never stopped praying." Rin always tried to hide it, knowing how Grey felt about prayer, but Grey had heard her whispering sometimes at night. Maybe her kid sister was the one who'd gotten it right after all.

If I go up to the heavens, you are there.

Sue Alexander stood and approached a cabinet on the wall. She removed a clean but stained hand towel, wet a corner of it from a canteen hanging on the back of a chair, and returned to Grey. Without a word, her mother gently wiped her face of the caked-on blood and dirt. She caressed her daughter with her other hand.

Grey closed her eyes as the cool cloth soothed her eyelids. It had been so long since she'd slept.

"You're beautiful," Mom said.

"I've got a fat lip."

Her mother chuckled.

"Rin's the pretty one. You'll see, she . . . she's . . . I looked after her, Mom. I don't know what I'll do if . . ."

Mom helped Grey lie down on the cot and placed a warm blanket over her. "I love you," she whispered.

32

As the entrance to the dome slammed shut behind them, Rin flinched. They walked past rows of cells with tiny openings in the doors, and her nose wrinkled at the smell of human excrement wafting out of them. Through the bars, Rin could see fearful eyes staring back at her.

What was this place?

"Over here," the guard said.

Was she being led to her death? She felt like an animal caught in a cruel trap. She could feel the skin around her ankle oozing, and Rin labored to keep pace with the soldiers and Dana.

She was just beginning to like Dana too.

They marched past the cell blocks to where several military personnel sat at tables eating or playing card games. The soldiers eyed them. Dana's back stiffened at their stares, but her escorts didn't linger. Instead, they walked Rin and Dana straight through the room and down a dark corridor. At an unmarked door, the first guard swiped his hand across a reader. Swinging it open, he waved them inside.

Rin hesitated but was quickly pushed forward into a cold, white room. She found herself squinting under glaring lights. Goose bumps quickly popped up on her arms.

One wall had shelves packed with an assortment of medical supplies and instruments—bandages, tape, bottles of pills, and small vials of liquid. Several stainless-steel examination tables lined the center of the room. Without sheets or mattresses, she shivered at the thought of lying on one of them. Was this a morgue or a hospital? Dangling under the tables, Rin caught sight of thick, canvas restraints.

Across the room a huddle of Mazdaar uniforms were talking. Rin couldn't make out their words, but she saw Dana eyeing the tall woman with the spiky blonde hair in the center. General Evangeline Yurkutz turned toward them, and Rin tried to force down her boiling hatred at the sight of her. This woman had tortured Grey and manipulated Dad. Had the woman's eyes widened slightly when she saw Dana?

Flexing her fingers behind her back to try and regain some feeling, Rin wondered what Grey had first felt when she faced her. Even outside the zones, everyone knew *of* Yurkutz, but seeing her face-to-face was terrifying.

With a snap of her fingers, Yurkutz ordered all but one of her drone guards out of the space, and before Rin knew it she was alone with the drone, Dana, and her mother in the creepy medical room.

"I brought you a present," Dana said, tilting her head toward Rin.

Yurkutz searched her daughter with those weird, yellow eyes. "Six years," she said.

Dana lifted her chin. "Yes, I'm all grown up."

"Scan her," the general ordered the drone.

As if expecting the move, Dana spread her legs and raised her arms as the drone approached, waving its hands over her body. They were probably equipped with weapon-detecting sensors.

Dana's eyes remained fixed on her mother.

"Clear," the drone said.

Dana dropped her arms. "There's no way they'll stay in hiding if you've got both of their children."

Yurkutz approached Rin.

"Where is my sister?" she demanded, refusing to allow herself to be afraid.

The woman glanced at Dana. "You could learn something from these Alexanders. They are loyal to a fault." Grabbing Rin by the chin, she towered over her. "Your sister learned the hard way what happens to those who resist me."

Rin gritted her teeth. "What have you done to her?"

Yurkutz's fingernails dug into Rin's face as she turned toward Dana. "She will be useful."

"Mother, I—"

The general let Rin go and swung around abruptly to Dana. "You, however . . ." She gave her daughter another long, scrutinizing look-over. "Do you honestly think you can come back to me as if nothing happened? They've poisoned you for my purposes."

Dana took in a deep breath. "I never believed them."

After everything her parents and Mrs. March had done, how could Dana say that? How could she have fooled all of them?

"I won them over. They trusted me. I can take you to them."

"I already know where they are."

What?

Dana paused. "Their forces are next to nil, their defenses

minimal." She squared her shoulders. "Mother, I can help you defeat Yien."

General Yurkutz smiled, and Rin's blood chilled.

·⧓·

The assembly took place in the main gallery, the first room Grey had seen when she'd entered her mother's foreign world. Five of the cylindrical lanterns containing the fiery liquid hung from the walls, their glow bright enough to create the illusion of sunlight and reveal stalactites hanging from the ceiling far above them.

Mom followed Grey's stare to the nearest lantern. "They're fueled with water."

"Water?"

"Not like Earth's. There's a petroleum element in its composition. We have to filter it to drink it. Takes getting used to, I know. Everything about this planet does."

Grey wanted to ask her about the Tasmanian wolves again and the mighty wind gusts, but the meeting was about to start. As everyone's eyes turned toward her, Grey felt their suspicion. Did they think she was with Mazdaar like Lee?

"I'll wait over there." She pointed toward the far wall where she could melt into the background. Her arm throbbed, and she still felt sick to her stomach over the idea of human bodies being turned into drones.

"Stay with me," Mom said.

It was as much a command as any Mom had given Pierce. Grey edged closer to her mother. Together they walked up to a table at the front. Pierce finger-whistled, and the rumble of conversation instantly ceased. It looked like every one of the fifty people living in this place had shown up. Some appeared as old as Mrs. March; a few were just children. Had all of the adults once been Mazdaar prisoners?

Captain Sue Alexander took a deep breath and visually swept the crowd. She held up her hand as the group asked a volley of ricocheting questions. "Please, let me say something first. Then I will answer everything."

Mom wrapped her arm around Grey, and she leaned against her, glad for her support. It still hadn't fully sunk in that her mother was alive.

"Many of you have heard me speak of my children," her mother began. "The hope of seeing them again has kept me going every day for the past five years. Today, one of my prayers was answered when God sent my oldest daughter, Grey, into our camp."

A collective murmur spread through the cavern.

"She has been a prisoner of Mazdaar," Mom continued. "They were using her to find Tanner and me." She went on to explain everything Grey had said about seeing her father on a conference screen, her time in Mazdaar City, General Yurkutz, and her journey to Jupiter. When Mom got to the part about the other prisoners and what Lee had revealed about their bodies being used to create drones, the group fell silent.

"They could be on their way to kill us now!" someone exclaimed.

Grey studied the stone floor, not wanting to meet anyone's eyes. Her very presence here was putting this whole group in danger. And once Mazdaar got what they wanted out of Dad, he was as good as dead too. He was willing to risk everything to save her, and Grey hated it.

The medic, Sharayah, pushed her way up to the front. "So what are our options?"

As far as Grey was concerned there was only one. She pictured the faces of the men and women on the *Genesis* flight—Paul and his lofty plans, the young couple in love, and every other person who'd boarded the ship hoping for adventure and a new life on Jupiter. They'd bought Mazdaar's lie, but they didn't deserve to die. No one did. Not even Lee.

"We can either pull out," Mom said, "or launch a rescue."

"They have five squadrons," Pierce said, stepping forward. "Not good odds for sure, but we know the landscape. They do not."

"We wouldn't have a chance!"

Grey swung around at Finley's booming voice. He pointed a thick finger at her mother's chest. "You'd risk every one of our lives for the minuscule chance of rescuing your husband?"

Pierce stepped in between Finley and Mom. "We're talking about over eighty prisoners."

Shoving the older man away, Finley's hands balled into fists. "I don't care who we're talking about! I'm not throwing my life away because of—"

"Enough!" Mom's command rang through the room. Grey remembered a time when she and Rin had been bickering and Mom had intervened, forcing them to apologize and make up.

Her mother—the woman who bore her, who'd recited those verses before bed and tucked them in every night—she didn't exist anymore, did she? Today Grey realized she was meeting her mother, her real mother, for the first time.

Grumbling turned to angry shouting, and the crowd pressed in. Even with every one of them, they'd barely make just one squadron. And they were all human. Mazdaar had inanimate drones that could keep fighting even when maimed.

Pierce stepped closer to Mom, the lanterns reflecting off his glasses. He'd been the voice of reason in the woods when Finley had wanted to kill her and Lee, and Mom seemed to respect him.

"I need everyone's attention . . . now!" Mom clapped, and the room instantly quieted. Her eyes closed for a moment.

When she opened them again, she looked straight at Grey. "I said we have two possible courses. I didn't say which one we are going to take."

Finley's broad chest heaved in and out, like he was ready for a fight, but he seemed to get hold of himself and at least listen to his superior.

Mom shook her head. "I know we would be risking everything to launch a rescue. I can't ask you to do that with our small numbers."

Grey stared at her mother.

"Everyone be ready to move out by nightfall, and we'll get as much distance between us and Orion settlement as we can."

"Wait. Mom, what are you *saying?*"

Sue Alexander reached for Grey. "Please listen to me. This isn't what I want. But I have to think of my duty to these people. I can't unnecessarily risk their lives any more than I can yours."

Panic bubbled inside her, and Grey searched for someone, anyone in the crowd who would take her side. "This isn't just about my father," she pleaded with them all. "Eighty people will die if we don't do something!"

"Yeah, and fifty of us'll die if we try!" a woman from the crowd shouted.

Grey attempted to infuse her voice with sympathy. She held up her wrists, hoping the others would see the marks from the shock cuffs. "I was a Mazdaar prisoner too. If we allow them to do this, we might as well surrender and join them, because we'll be just as bad. We'll be—"

"Grey, that's enough." Mom pulled her aside, away from the front.

She twisted out of her mother's grasp. "Don't you *care* about Dad?"

"I love him just as much as you do." Sue Alexander's eyes were moist. "But we don't have a chance against that many."

"We have to try!"

"I'll lose both of you if we go." Mom rested her hand on Grey's shoulder. "I'm so sorry, but we can't save him. Do you really think he'd want us to try?"

"What about the others? They're all gonna die."

"And so will you, me, and everyone here." Her mother squeezed her shoulder with each word.

"He's there because of me." Grey almost crumpled from the weight of the guilt. All these years, all this time, and she was going to lose Dad all over again. She tried to control herself as her mother dismissed the people with the order to prepare for movement. Mom walked her outside the cave where the clatter of preparations dimmed. When it was just the two of them, Mom tried to hug her.

Grey stiffened. Mom and all these people were giving up on Dad and allowing Mazdaar to win. Innocent people were going to suffer. Then Grey suddenly clung to her mother. Up until now, Mazdaar had stolen everything from her, but at least she had her mom again.

"It is not your fault, and your father would never want you to think that," Mom whispered into her hair.

Grey lifted her eyes toward the buttes surrounding them, remembering how many times she and Rin had wondered how they would make it on their own. She pictured her little sister looking up to her, never doubting she'd protect them. When she was with Rin, Grey always found a way.

"I can't just leave those people."

"You don't have a—"

"Yes, I do." She pulled away, desperate to find understanding on her mother's face.

Before her mother could respond, a blast of wind surged

over them like a wave. Grey saw hundreds of swirling dust devils swerving first one way, then the other, intersecting and mingling into a massive maelstrom.

"Cover your eyes!" Mom said above the roar, pulling Grey into the shelter of the doorway.

Grey did, but she inhaled a cloud of dust before she could protect her mouth. She coughed violently. "What . . . causes it?" Grey finally managed. She risked a peek outside and couldn't see the buttes anymore through the swirling dirt and sand.

"Probably the gases above the clouds, but we don't know for sure," her mom shouted.

Then, just like in the woods, the air currents ceased as abruptly as they began. Grey coughed again, then stepped back outside and watched the dust settle. Any tracks they'd made would now be obliterated.

She heard a deep rustling and glanced up as the sky suddenly darkened and a huge shadow passed overhead.

"Get back." Mom yanked her into the doorway again.

"What is it?"

Her mother pointed, and a huge black bird dove toward where she'd been standing.

Grey had seen condors in the Preserve with nine-foot wingspans, but the size of this bird—if it could even be called that—left her speechless. Its body alone was larger than the boulder marking their silo entrance.

"Their wingspan can be over twenty-five feet," Mom said. "And they prey on anything that moves. Luckily, we don't see them often. Only after the winds."

The gigantic raptor swooped past, darkening the cave entrance even as several more dove from the clouds. They flew together in formation, banking first one way, then the other, searching the ground for their next meal.

Grey leaned closer to Mom. Long after the flock was gone, they remained huddled in the safety of the doorway.

"I wouldn't be able to live with myself if I don't try to help those people," Grey finally said.

Mom let out a long breath. "You are your father's daughter," she said softly. With a sigh she pulled a radio from her belt. "Pierce, I need you out here."

He immediately appeared along with two others and gave Mom a small salute.

"Take her to lockup," Mom said, gesturing to her daughter.

Grey jumped back. "What?"

"It's for your own good."

The men surrounded Grey.

Sue Alexander backed away, wiping at her eyes. "Do not hurt her." Then to Grey she said, "I can't lose you again, sweetheart."

33

"Where is my sister?" Rin asked, trying to keep her voice from quavering.

General Yurkutz didn't even look at her.

With her arms still tied behind her back, Rin took a step toward her and Dana. Instantly, the drone grabbed her by the hair. Rin yelped in pain.

"Let her go," the general ordered, and the drone obeyed.

For a moment, all Rin could hear was the pounding of blood in her head as she tried to stand steady in front of Yurkutz, the woman who'd ripped her family away from her. She knew it made her look weak to cry, and she fought it with all she had.

"What have you done to her? I have to know."

"Do you now?" The Mazdaar general laughed, and Dana joined in. "Look around you, Alexander girl. You are alone, just as your sister was."

Was? Oh, dear God, please.

Yurkutz seemed to regard Rin for a moment, one eyebrow piqued and both hands on her hips. "If you must know," she said in a mocking tone. She shoved Rin across the cold floor toward the steel tables. "Then you shall."

"Is she dead?"

"She might wish she was."

Rin tried to ward off mental images of her sister being shocked or worse, but as they approached the closest examination table, fear locked her limbs in place. She could pretend to be brave, but she'd heard what Mazdaar did to prisoners.

She tried not to look at the restraints under the table, but her eyes were glued to them. Yurkutz was right. There were some things worse than death.

The Lord is my shepherd, I shall not want.

Yurkutz pushed her up against the steel table, and the edge caught Rin in the stomach. She braced against it. She wasn't going down without a fight. Had Grey been able to withstand the torture for long?

Breath tickled her ear. "Watch and learn, girl."

A double door flew open, and several medics marched in carrying a limp man by the arms and legs. He was naked, and Rin averted her eyes in embarrassment.

Twisting her chin, General Yurkutz forced her to look. "I said *watch*."

The medics brought the man over to the table. With one quick movement, they threw him up onto the steel slab with a thud. She focused on his face and unseeing eyes, swallowing down her gag reflex. When she saw the singed hair on his dark chest, she realized how the man had died.

"I present to you Captain Victor Hertzog." With one finger, Yurkutz roughly lifted one of the man's eyelids, then the other.

Rin's stomach turned. Once in the Preserve she and Grey

had come across a dead antelope the vultures were devouring, but Grey had made her turn away. That was the closest thing to a dead body she'd ever seen.

"This man is an example to many."

"What did he do?" Dana asked, and Rin noticed she had taken a step away from the table. Rin wished she could too. The dead man's foot was inches from her.

Yurkutz waved toward the body. "He defied us. Defied *me.*"

She snapped her fingers, and two bulky drones entered. Between them walked a white-haired African man with sunken eyes. A raw scrape discolored his forehead.

"Ah, Dr. Lenoir!" Spinning on her heels, the general greeted him with a sneer.

The hunched man stopped in his tracks, causing the drones to bump into him. They latched onto his arms and dragged him across the room. He shook out of their grasp when he got to Yurkutz.

"You couldn't let him rest in peace," the man named Dr. Lenoir said, looking like he wanted to strangle the general.

"Rest?" Yurkutz chuckled. "Far from it. No, Doctor, my use of the venerable Hertzog isn't complete. What he would not do in life, he will do now."

Dr. Lenoir's eyes flared. "What wickedness is this?"

"I think you know."

The medics wheeled over two rattling carts. One contained large vials of an unknown dark-green fluid and several electronic devices the size of coins. The other was covered with shiny instruments lined up in rows. There were blades of various sizes, but Rin almost threw up when she spotted the saw.

Dr. Lenoir's face blanched. "And if I refuse?"

General Yurkutz prodded Rin in the back, and she felt

one of the woman's pointed nails dig into her flesh. "Then she will die."

··

Grey resisted the entire way to lockup. She was rewarded with sore muscles and raw knuckles.

Pierce closed her into one of the holding cells they'd apparently fashioned from wood and scrap metal. "Sorry, kid," he said. Waving off the other guards, he pulled a stool up to the cell. "I've known Sue for five years. And I've watched her pray every day."

She glared at the man.

"For you and your sister." Pierce gave her a sad smile. "That someday you'd be reunited, that you'd be safe. I thought she was delusional, yet here you are."

"Right. Here I am. A prisoner of my own mother."

"You are not a prisoner."

She grasped the bars of the cell. "I guess these are just my imagination."

Pierce stood. "You're an Alexander. You fight for those you love, even to the point of death. Your mother knows that and wants you to live."

"My father is going to die because of me!"

"He is an Alexander too."

"Isn't there anything you can do to help him?"

He waved toward the cavern's entrance. "We are few here. We cannot take on the Mazdaar army."

"Instead, you're going to run like cowards and let them make drones from the bodies of innocent people."

Pierce ran his fingers through his mop of hair. "Your bravery is admirable, girl. But walking away doesn't always make someone a coward. You'd do well to remember that."

With those words, he left Grey alone. She quickly examined her cell, searching for any vulnerability. The floor was stone, the bars thick, wooden beams. No way to break them. She focused on the lock. Its ancient design and the fact that it actually needed a key might make it easier to pick.

Grey shook the bars as hard as she could, not really expecting them to break from the force, but more to get a feel for their strength. No way was the door budging, either.

Slumping to the floor, she held her head in her hands. She needed to think. Mom obviously knew her better than she thought and had guessed what she wanted to do. But how could she actually lock up her own daughter? It was infuriating.

Grey stood and began pacing the small cell. Mom would probably try to bring her to her senses at some point, later today maybe. Grey took note that she'd grown to almost the same height as her mother, and she had youth on her side. But Mom had experience and probably all kinds of combat training. Did she dare try to physically overpower her own mother? No, she couldn't do that.

With a sigh, Grey stuffed her hands into her pockets, wincing at the fresh sting from the wound on her arm. She'd probably opened it up again struggling with the men.

Her fingers brushed against something metal deep in her pocket. Grey jerked her hand out and stared down at the small, metal device lying in her palm.

Dr. Lenoir's skelette.

34

Rin stared at the corpse on the metal slab. His skin was the color of a dark storm cloud; his mouth gaped as if in one final plea for mercy.

"The great Mazdaar," Dr. Lenoir said, "picking on children and old men."

Evangeline Yurkutz laughed. "Don't let him deceive you," she whispered to Rin loud enough for all to hear. "He pretends to be a fool, but if it wasn't for the great Dr. Lenoir we would not be here today."

Rin focused on the doctor's face. The corners of his mouth drooped, and his eyes seemed dull and watery.

"I am no longer proud of my past achievements. The Gihern chips were destroyed, so I do not know what you want me to—"

"We have the chip, Doctor."

Dr. Lenoir blinked several times, looking as shocked as Rin felt. "But . . . how?"

Yurkutz smiled. "Shall we continue, or will I have to convince you by other means?"

Rin felt herself breathing faster as it sunk in just what was going on here. All the equipment, apparatus, fluids. This dead man. But hadn't her father destroyed his research *and* the chip prototypes?

"Untie her," Dr. Lenoir snapped. "Or I will not work."

Surprisingly, Yurkutz gestured for Dana to do so, and Dana quickly complied.

"She'll be no good to us dead," Dana muttered.

With the grace of a lioness, Yurkutz closed the space between herself and Dana, glaring down at her daughter. "I did not ask your opinion."

Dana looked away.

Dr. Lenoir stepped up to the table, still shadowed by the drones. He nodded to Rin. "What is your name, dear?"

She would say it proudly. "Orinda Alexander."

The doctor's eyebrows rose. "Any relation to Grey Alexander?"

"She's my sister. How do you—"

Dana smacked the side of Rin's head. Fire flew down her neck as it snapped back, and she wondered if Dana was being particularly brutal to impress her mother.

"I just wanna know if she's alive!" Rin braced herself against the table and recoiled when her hand touched the cold leg of the dead man.

"You will be silent," the general said.

She nodded, rubbing her neck.

"Begin, Doctor."

Sighing, the old man snapped on rubber gloves and approached the carts. For a moment, he balked. He slowly picked up a scalpel. It glinted under the lights. "It was once my life's goal to make a drone from a human body," he muttered.

"Now I would give anything to take back those years of work. And for your information, your sister got away," Dr. Lenoir quietly added.

Dana swung toward her mother. "You let her escape?"

The doctor gave Rin an almost imperceptible nod.

"I said begin," Yurkutz growled.

Grey made sure the guards were gone before she tried the skelette. Reaching through the bars, she let it hover over the lock, and it quickly warmed. Something clicked, and the lock popped open.

Grey carefully dropped the skelette back into her pocket and stepped from the cell. She listened. Clattering and shuffling. A metallic squeaking. Everyone would be busy packing up for their massive retreat. Her only chance to steal away undetected would be to act like she belonged.

And if she didn't run into Pierce or her mother.

Taking in a deep breath to calm her nerves, she flipped through her options. If Mom found her now, she'd search her and take away the skelette. Grey would never have another chance to save the prisoners—or her father. She had to get away or forever live with the guilt of knowing she hadn't done all she could.

She silently slipped out of the chamber. Lanterns were spaced about ten feet apart and illuminated the stone floor that was littered with reddish pebbles and the dust of a hundred boots. Her arm still ached, but she made herself march confidently and turn down the passage like she knew exactly where she was going. And she did this time. She just hoped Mom would be busy supervising somewhere else.

Someone rushed toward her carrying a stack of metal bins. Grey pretended she didn't notice him and barely breathed as he passed, the edge of one of the bins bumping her shoulder. She could smell his sweat.

"You there!"

Grey froze, squelching the urge to run. A second set of feet pounded on the stone floor, and a dark-skinned woman rushed toward Grey. Had she been recognized?

Grey braced as the woman skidded to a stop in front of her. She was sweating too and huffed in air like she wasn't used to rushing around.

"Did a man just pass you with a stack of boxes?" the woman asked.

Grey's shoulders relaxed slightly. They must not have heard that Mom had locked her up.

"Down there." She pointed in the direction she'd come.

"Okay, great. Thanks!" The woman took off down the corridor away from her, and Grey started walking again, this time a little faster.

Stopping at her mother's quarters, Grey decided on one detour. She strained to hear any voices inside. When she heard nothing, she popped in.

Empty.

She rushed over to the table, and sure enough, the black coilgun she had seen earlier still lay where her mother had left it. Grey snatched it up, stuffing it into her waistband and making sure her tunic kept it hidden.

One more hurdle to go. There'd be people in that main gallery, but Grey had to chance it. She walked straight into the bustle where people called out to each other and passed containers, bags, and machinery.

Go. Don't look back.

When she reached the chameleon-cloth-covered exit, Grey forced herself to pass through. She blinked against the sudden daylight and took a moment to stare up at the crazy, swirling sky before she took off running across the Jupiter terrain. She couldn't think about never seeing her mother again or that she was probably going to die on this planet sooner rather than later.

35

Rin watched in horror as Dr. Lenoir performed the procedure on the body of Victor Hertzog. He replaced the man's blood with a green solution he called glutaraldehyde, his heart with a biopump, and then planted four coin-sized electronic chips at the base of each limb.

Perspiration beaded on Dr. Lenoir's forehead as he closed the last incision with a layer of self-healing bioskin. He narrated his movements as he went through the operation, presumably for her benefit and maybe for his own. When he was nearly done, he explained how the Gehirn chip needed to be planted last at the base of the man's brain. Dr. Lenoir picked up the miniature circular saw and approached the end of the table where the man's head lay.

"Turn him over," the doctor said, and Yurkutz waved for the two medics to obey the man. This time, Rin did close her eyes. But she still heard the exact moment when the saw met bone.

He's dead. He's dead. He's dead. He can't feel anything.

They brought in the connecting equipment, and Rin was forced to watch as they tested the viability of the chips, causing each of the man's limbs to move independently. But it was when they came to the brain chip that her stomach lurched again.

Dr. Lenoir gave her a tired, sympathetic glance as he pressed the button to connect the final chip. His finger pressed the key floating on the virtual keyboard beside him, and the dead man's eyelids slowly opened, revealing huge, dilated pupils.

"Is he . . . dangerous?" Dana asked.

Yurkutz laughed. "Of course he is."

Dr. Lenoir pressed a few more keys, then stepped away from the table, peeling off his gloves. "I patched him into your server. It will take him a few hours to fully function."

Yurkutz crossed her arms, surveying the body. "We have your father to thank for this moment, Orinda."

Rin glared at Yurkutz.

"Oh, yes. Dear old dad and Mazdaar used to be"—Yurkutz entwined two fingers together—"like this. Did you know that?"

"Until he found out how evil you really were," Rin managed, expecting to pay for the remark.

Dana moved to strike her, but her mother held her off with an upraised hand.

Yurkutz's eyes bored through Rin. "Your father broke every one of his promises to Mazdaar. He stole from us the greatest invention our world has ever known, and you dare to call *us* evil?"

Rin eyed the body, remembering everything Mrs. March had told her. This is exactly why she thought Dad had destroyed the chip, and pride welled inside Rin.

"But fortunately for us," Yurkutz said. "Tanner Alexander had the chance to redeem himself once and for all."

Rin straightened. "Dad would never—"

The Mazdaar general smiled. "Oh, but he already has."

The dome loomed in front of Grey.

She crouched at the base of one of the trees and watched the sentry at the entrance. Even from this distance, she could see his metallic hands.

She surveyed the entrance, and her hope faded. This was a formidable machine guarding the door. His eyes never stopped scanning, and she knew that the moment she stepped into the clearing he would alert and probably take her down with one blast of his blueflare.

She pulled out her coilgun and stared at the short barrel. No way could she make the shot. Not at this range. There had to be a different way in.

Painstakingly, she snuck from twisted tree to twisted tree, inching her way toward the rear of the huge edifice where she spotted another smaller door, this one seemingly unguarded. Why would they guard one entrance and not the other? Was it monitored electronically instead?

There was no way to know, but it was her only option. The best plan she'd been able to formulate was to break in and release as many of the prisoners as she could using the skelette before the guards took her out. If she freed enough people before they killed her, maybe they could fight their way to the woods.

Grey braced herself for the spring to the entrance. Then she ran straight across the clearing, zeroing in on her target. She reached it within seconds and held the skelette over the lock.

Nothing happened.

Grey muttered an oath and tried again. Her hands shook, but this time the skelette turned hot in her hand. She quickly turned the doorknob and stepped inside. Her life was almost over.

The back room was full of freight containers stacked to the ceiling with only a small aisle between them. It was wide enough for walking but with barely enough light to see where she was going. How could this room be unguarded? Had she tripped a silent alarm?

She didn't take time to ponder her luck and headed down the aisle, trying to remember what she could about the layout of the dome. She had to get to the cells.

Grey jogged down the aisle, amazed when she reached the door at the far end of the room without confronting anyone.

Then the door opened.

36

You seem surprised, Orinda." A slight grin came to General Yurkutz's lips.

Rin could only stare at the general. Dad had redeemed himself? What did that mean?

Yurkutz turned toward her daughter. "Remember me telling you these Alexanders are loyal to a fault? Tanner is the epiphany of that trait."

"He would die before he gave in to you," Rin muttered.

"But he would not let his children die." With a flick of her hand, Yurkutz ordered Dr. Lenoir and the medics escorted out, leaving Rin alone with Dana and her mother. She wished to be anywhere but here. Anywhere.

Yurkutz stood directly in front of Dana. "Why do you come to me now?"

Anywhere but here.

Dana seemed to struggle to pull her eyes from the twitching bio-drone on the table. In her dusty, tan flight suit, she looked diminished standing next to her mother in her crisp, Mazdaar uniform.

"I—"

"Everything was within your grasp." General Yurkutz came to stand directly in front of Dana. "Yet you threw it all away. For what?"

"I have information," Dana said.

"What information could you possibly give us that we don't already have?"

"Fleur March is alive."

Yurkutz's eyes blazed. "Do not lie to me."

"She's here, on Jupiter."

"Here?"

"She flew us in."

A curse slipped from the Mazdaar general's lips. "We will deal with her later."

"What about Tanner?" Dana said softly.

Yurkutz snapped her fingers twice, and a guard poked his head in the room.

"General?" he said with a salute.

"Bring in Tanner Alexander," Yurkutz said.

❖

Grey froze, like an exhausted jackrabbit scared out of her wits.

A Mazdaar soldier stepped into the storeroom, his massive form backlit by the lights in the corridor. He closed the door and at first didn't seem to notice her. Grey gripped her gun with both hands. There was nowhere to run. She would have to kill or be killed, as if she was back in the Preserve facing that border patroller all over again.

She raised her weapon as the guard turned. He saw her.

Grey's finger tightened over the trigger.

"Hey!"

His voice was higher than she expected, cracking when he shouted. His hand flew to the laser strapped to his thigh.

If she didn't act fast, he'd alert the whole compound. Grey aimed for his chest, right where she'd shot the patroller.

The soldier's weapon cleared its sheath.

Now! It was a clear shot.

But Grey's hands felt like they were made of stone. What if this guard had been forced here? What if he had family back home waiting for him to come back alive?

He swung his weapon toward her face, and two back-to-back shots came before Grey could blink. She flinched, expecting searing pain, but it never came. Instead, the man fell to the floor, his weapon clattering on the concrete.

Grey swung around. The door she had come in stood ajar, and walking toward her with a violetflare laser still trained on the fallen soldier was Captain Sue Alexander.

37

"Mom! What are you—"

"Quickly, shut the door." Mom's voice was barely audible.

Grey rushed around her and obeyed. She returned to find her mother crouched down by the fallen guard, her fingers pressed against his neck.

"Is he?"

"Yes. We have to move now, Grey. Take his weapon."

Mom placed the guard's violetflare in Grey's trembling hand, and for a moment their eyes locked. It was hard to believe it had only been hours since she'd found Mom standing in that cave, the confident leader of a group of refugees.

"You weren't supposed to come after me."

Mom checked the levels of her own laser and scanned the huge containers surrounding them. "How many times have you needed me and I haven't been there?"

"They'll kill us."

"You knew that when you came."

She swallowed hard, trying to keep her voice down. "I couldn't just let them—"

"I know, sweetheart. I know. But we don't have a chance standing here talking. Do you know where the prisoners are housed?"

Grey tried to describe where she thought she'd been held with the Lenoirs. She showed her mother the skelette. "If we free enough of them, maybe they can help us."

But her mother was already shaking her head. "They'll be shot before they can get out the doors."

"Then what—"

"How many drones have you seen?"

"I'm not sure." She thought back to when she was inside *Genesis*. There had been dozens. "Fifty, maybe?"

"Mazdaar cosmoships are equipped with servers." Her mother stepped over the dead guard, edging toward the door he'd come through. "But when they get down here on Jupiter, they probably transfer to something more permanent. If we can locate and destroy that, the prisoners might have a chance. It will at least eliminate some of the guards."

"But won't they just switch the drones back to the server on the ship?"

Mom reached for the door handle, holding her finger to her lips. "There might be just enough of a delay. And shipboard servers would have severely limited range. If they can run fast enough, they might make it."

Grey was acutely aware that her mother said *they*, not *we*. Which meant she knew as well as Grey did that their own chance of survival was minimal. Because of her foolishness, she'd just sentenced her mother to die along with her.

Without thinking, she quickly grabbed her mother into one last desperate hug.

Mom smelled like the dusty Jupiter field they'd both crossed to get here.

"I'm sorry," Grey whispered.

Mom held her tight. Then they both pulled away and re-gripped their weapons. There was no time to cry, no time for good-byes. No way to make up for the years they'd lost and the future they'd never have.

"We're together," Mom said. "That's what counts."

"Tanner is *here?*" Dana asked.

Evangeline Yurkutz stood rigid and in control. "He turned himself in yesterday. Smart man."

Rin wanted to crumple to the floor. If Dad was here and thought Grey's life was in danger, he would've done anything Yurkutz asked. Mazdaar had all the equipment, and they no doubt knew what supplies he'd need. He would have given them the chip to save Grey.

She felt sick staring at the bio-drone. And now that Yurkutz had it, how long before Rin had to watch the cruel leader kill her family and Mrs. March?

When three drones marched into the medical room, her father between them, Rin ran to him.

"Dad!"

He lifted his bound hands, and she threw herself under them and into his embrace. For a moment nothing existed but the two of them, and Rin held on as her father silently rocked her. He'd make everything okay, wouldn't he? Things would be all right now. They had to be.

"My little Rinny," he whispered. "They got you, too."

She stared up at his bearded face. "Grey got away."

His eyes widened, probably wondering how much his daughter knew, before one of the drones yanked her away from him. Its metallic fingers pinched Rin's neck, contorting her head at a painful angle.

Yurkutz approached. "Tanner Alexander, we meet again."

"Yes," was all her father said.

"I knew you wouldn't let me down."

"I had no choice."

"Because you had to save your daughter," the general mocked.

"Exactly like you planned it."

A smile that was anything but kind tugged at the general's lips. She waved toward Hertzog's body. "The fruit of your labor."

Rin saw her father view the corpse lying motionless on the steel table. "Let my daughter go."

"Which one?" The general reached over and tried to stroke Rin's cheek with the back of her fingers.

Rin recoiled.

"I'd hate for anything to mar your daughter's pretty face."

Dad struggled against his captors, but they held him back firmly.

"You aren't quite finished," Yurkutz said in a low tone. "And if you aren't willing to oblige, I will force you to watch things happen to your daughter that no father should ever have to see."

Grey silently crept out into the empty hallway, crouching behind her mother. Mom used hand signals to direct their way.

They slipped past two doors with fingerprint sensors. Mom waved them forward, right as a door beside Grey flung open and a drone with a metal forehead stepped out into the hallway.

Grey didn't hesitate this time and fired directly at its chest.

It had no time to speak before it dropped, its twisted body propping the door open.

Shouts erupted from the room, and Grey gave Mom a frantic look. They took off down the corridor at a dead run. She heard someone yell—a girl—and her heart almost stopped. She *knew* that voice!

Grey took no time to think. She dove back toward the metal heap of a drone, knowing it would haunt her forever if she didn't. She pushed aside the body, green fluid oozing from its chest, and burst through the door even as her mother shouted for her to stop.

Her gun in both hands, Grey thought she was poised for anything, but what she saw almost didn't register.

Dad.

Rin.

And standing with their own weapons drawn and pointed straight at her were two more drones, their dilated eyes fixed and ready to kill.

"Hold your fire," a woman ordered, and that's when Grey spotted General Yurkutz standing next to a stainless-steel examination table where a naked Captain Hertzog lay sprawled, his limbs shaking. The horror of what was happening sunk in.

"Grey!"

She jerked toward the voice. Rin stood helplessly beside the general and another girl Grey didn't recognize. She looked unharmed, but Grey suddenly knew all she'd done to try and protect her little sister had been for naught.

Mom rushed into the room just behind her with her violetflare outstretched.

"Well, well." Yurkutz stepped forward. "A family reunion."

38

General Yurkutz moved toward Grey. "I would suggest you lose the lasers." The general had an MI pistol aimed at them. "Or I guarantee I will kill someone you love today."

If she took a shot at her, would Mom get the drones? Grey glanced at Dad, and he shook his head ever so slightly as if he could read her thoughts.

She reluctantly set her weapon on the ground, and her mother did the same beside her.

"Rinny. Tanner," Mom whispered.

The Alexander family faced each other, two on each side of the room, separated by a chasm that was Mazdaar. Mom's body shook, as if it took all her energy to keep herself from running over and holding Rin and her husband.

"Looks like you finally got what you wanted, Evangeline," Mom said.

The Mazdaar general chuckled. "Not quite."

"It's me you want." Dad tried to take a step forward, but

the drone's massive arm crushed around his torso. As a little girl, Grey never doubted for a moment he would protect her. And that's exactly why he'd come here, wasn't it? Now the only man she'd ever felt safe with was as trapped and helpless as she was.

Yurkutz studied each of them. She turned toward the girl Grey didn't know. "They make a unique study, don't they? Archaic, yet unique. Perhaps we should test their loyalty further."

"Mother, I don't—"

Mother?

"No," Dad said. "I will do anything, but just let my family go."

Grey was surprised at the strength in her father's voice.

"You're right, Tanner. You will." The general cocked her head toward the drones, probably sending them orders through her Dot. "But do you honestly think I will release them now? I thought you knew me better than that." She turned toward the girl Grey realized was her daughter. "Dana, you will take Tanner and lock him up with the other prisoners. I want to have a chat with his little family."

Dad struggled futilely against the drones as the young woman named Dana brushed past Grey. Mom's eyes were full of rage as she watched them restrain her husband. She took one step toward him but then stopped herself as if she realized it would only endanger him.

The drones shoved him toward the door. "I love you, Sue!" Dad said over his shoulder, straining to keep his wife in view. "And you girls! Stay strong."

Desperation tinged his voice. When the door slammed shut behind them, Grey glanced at Rin. Her lower lip trembled.

Yurkutz moved toward Grey, the MI held loosely in her fingers, the remaining drone a stoic guard beside her. From the moment Mazdaar had snatched Grey from the Preserve, this woman had used her for one thing—to find her parents. She knew they would do anything to save their children, and by the looks of Captain Hertzog, Dad already had. If the general threatened Grey or Rin with the MI now, Mom would be putty in her hands too. Grey had to take a chance the MI was set to stun.

It was now or never.

Grey lunged at Yurkutz, shoving her with all her strength. Muscle thunked against bone, and the general stumbled backward. Grey fought to grab the MI, but the general overpowered her so quickly she barely knew what was happening. This time, instead of throwing Grey to the floor, Yurkutz twisted her closer and jammed the MI against her chest.

Grey kicked and floundered against her.

The MI hummed.

Yurkutz fired.

The shock Grey felt was nothing like the tortuous pain she'd experienced with the cuffs. It zapped straight to her core and seemed to permeate every tissue, every muscle, every cell, even her heart itself. She felt herself shudder and fall as the room blackened. She couldn't move. Couldn't breathe.

"Grey!"

It was Rin's voice, and Grey's confused consciousness couldn't place where she was. Was she back in the Preserve in a deep sleep?

"No! What did you do to her? Please don't die, Grey. Please."

She tried to inhale. She could breathe. Where was she? As her eyes began to function again, she tried to get up. Rin quickly helped her to her feet.

Suddenly, an explosion rocketed through the room. The glass panels on the medical cabinets shattered, and Grey and

Rin fell back to the ground as a wall caved in and filled the room with white smoke.

Grey choked and tried to blink away the dust and make sense of the chaos. What was happening? Had Mazdaar blown something up?

Through the haze, Grey could see the drone and Hertzog's body crushed under a piece of concrete wall and Yurkutz and Mom struggling in hand-to-hand combat, punching and parrying and drawing blood.

Mom blocked a kick from the general with both hands, then spun and shot a drop-kick of her own. It connected with Yurkutz's side, sending a guttural oath through her teeth. Yurkutz ducked to the side to avoid another kick and thrust a fist toward Mom's nose.

Jumping backward, Mom avoided the punch, but seconds later, took a crushing boot to the side of her head which sent her stumbling backward. She tripped on a piece of plaster that had fallen from the ceiling, landing on the cement floor with a thud.

The Mazdaar general was on her in a second, throwing another punch at Mom's face. But Mom rolled away just in time, pouncing back to her feet. A crimson stream flowed down her temple, but her eyes were on fire.

Grey frantically searched for a fallen weapon to help her mother, even as Rin flew toward Yurkutz, screaming bloody murder.

"Rin, no!"

Grey spotted a violetflare next to the medical table where Captain Hertzog's body still lay. She dove for the weapon, then pivoted back and fired at Yurkutz.

Yurkutz cried out as the beam hit her thigh, but she didn't drop.

"The next one's straight through your head!"

Another explosion shook the room from somewhere outside the dome, but Grey kept her aim steady. That's when she saw Rin lying crumpled on the ground. Mom, her chest heaving, blood and sweat dripping down her forehead, knelt beside her.

Her sister wasn't moving.

39

Is she okay?" Grey yelled to her mother.

Mom held Rin's face in her hands. "It was a heel kick to her chest. If it hit her heart, it could cause cardiac arrest. And she's not breathing!"

Grey lowered the gun to General Yurkutz's knee and pulled the trigger again. Her shot met its mark, and this time the Mazdaar general fell, cursing. The only thing keeping Grey from killing her right then was that it was exactly what someone like Yurkutz would do. She wouldn't allow herself to stoop to that level, but she wanted her to suffer for a few minutes. A medic could patch up her wounds later, and someone else could decide whether she lived or died.

"Come on, Rinny," Mom begged. "Come back to us!"

Her mother's tone sent panic straight through Grey. She edged closer to them, still keeping the weapon trained on Yurkutz, who was trying to clutch her bloody leg and knee at the same time. She was no doubt calling for reinforcements through her Dot. How much time did they have before the general's daughter or more soldiers returned?

A third, fainter explosion reverberated through the walls. Were those the redflare cannons? If Mazdaar was firing them, what was going on? Was the settlement under attack? They had to get out of here before another wall caved in.

Grey knelt on the floor, reaching for Rin's neck. Pressing her fingers against the carotid artery, she prayed her worst fears weren't coming true. God wouldn't let it end like this, would He?

"I can't feel a pulse!" Grey's words came out in a shriek. When Yurkutz tried to get up, Grey pulled herself away from Rin and hovered over the general. She knew it was wrong to hate like this, but the feeling roiled up inside her with the intensity of a solar flare.

General Evangeline Yurkutz raised herself up onto her good leg and stared at Grey. Even wounded, venom spewed from her eyes. "You Alexanders think you're invincible. But you know what? You're a bunch of weak, bleeding hearts."

Grey looked back at Rin. Her sister lay motionless on the dirty floor of a Jupiter medical lab. Her mother, who'd spent five years praying for their reconciliation, was desperately performing chest compressions on the daughter she hadn't seen grow up. And Dad? He was locked away, maybe even dead.

Grey raised the laser to the woman's head, her finger twitching on the trigger. "What did we ever do to you?" She was practically screaming.

Yurkutz didn't have time to answer.

The door to the lab exploded open, and a team of masked soldiers clad in body armor and brandishing thick blueflare rifles shot through the door and methodically fanned through the room before Grey could shoot. The symbol of a yellow rising sun was stitched on their black uniforms, and white stripes ran down their sleeves. She'd only seen this symbol one other time—on Jet—in the High Council chamber where he'd defended her.

"Stand down, girl."

It wasn't the order that stopped her. She hated this general enough to send the beam on its deadly course, but Grey suddenly wondered what Rin would think of her if she took an unarmed person's life.

"Grey, don't!"

A soldier came toward Grey. How did she know her name? Was this some sort of trick? Grey backed up, not taking any chances. "Stay where you are!"

"Hold your fire." It was the apparent leader who approached Grey.

"I said stay where you are, or I will kill her!" Grey aimed for Yurkutz once more.

Setting her rifle on the ground, the leader ripped off her face mask. White hair spilled to her shoulders. "Grey, it's me. You're safe."

The sight of Mrs. March was so unexpected that Grey didn't believe what she was seeing. Surely, this was just someone who resembled their elderly neighbor back home. Grey looked into the woman's kind face and gasped. She didn't know how it was possible, but it *was* Mrs. March. What in the world was she doing giving orders to Yien soldiers?

"Mrs March?"

Covering the ground between them with confident strides, Mrs. March quickly took the gun from Grey's hand.

"We've got to get you all out of here," Mrs. March said. "Yien forces are still securing the compound."

"Rin, she . . ."

But Mrs. March had already seen. As two of her men restrained Yurkutz, Mrs. March rushed over to where Mom was still trying to revive Rin. Mom breathed into Rin's mouth, then frantically began the compressions again.

"I need a medic over here," Mrs. March ordered. "Now!"

Mom shook her head, but she kept on. "It's too late."

Mrs. March knelt down beside her. "Don't give up, Sue. Don't."

Soldiers rushed over with a stretcher of some kind and scooped Rin onto it. Grey tried to push past Mrs. March and follow them as Mom rushed with them from the room still giving compressions. Mrs. March held Grey back.

"Let them do their job. I promise they'll do everything they can to help her."

Grey didn't have the strength to resist. Between the MI shock, her bandaged wound, and her plummeting adrenaline, she could barely stand.

"My sister has no pulse," she cried.

"It's not over yet. Have faith."

"In *what?*" She fought to keep herself from becoming hysterical, but Rin was dead or dying, and she couldn't do a thing about it. She'd given up everything to save her, but Mazdaar had won. Even if Yien's army could conquer the settlement, Rin would be gone. No matter how hard Grey fought against them, Mazdaar always won.

Mrs. March gripped her by the shoulders. "Have faith in the One who got us all here safely and who kept you and your parents alive for five years. That's W*ho* you need to have faith in, sweetheart, because through every one of these trials, He has *never* left your side."

She stared into Mrs. March's face, into those clear emerald eyes, and everything melted inside. She took in the full picture of her in Yien battle array. She was barely recognizable.

"How are you even here?"

"I'll explain, but first, where is your father?"

"They locked him up."

Mrs. March frowned. She touched her earplug. "Tanner's not here. Neither is Dana. I have Grey. Continue to search and secure the perimeter." Guiding her, Mrs. March stepped over the dead drone sprawled across the threshold and led them down the same corridor she and Mom had run through only minutes earlier. This time they headed in the opposite direction.

"I've been serving the Yien Dynasty for many years," Mrs. March said as they rushed. "I'm actually a commander in their special forces."

"What?"

"I had to be covert for the same reason your parents couldn't tell you about their involvement. A small group of us from the Preserve arrived on Jupiter a few hours ago using the ship in your silo," Mrs. March continued. "That's how Rin got here too. We were trying to figure out how to rescue both of you when Yien reinforcements arrived."

Grey stumbled, catching herself on the wall.

Rin had no pulse.

"The Yien Dynasty has been trying to claim Jupiter for years in order to keep it out of Mazdaar's hands, and this invasion is phase one." Mrs. March stopped running and held her hand to her ear again, as if listening. "Surprise was our only advantage," she continued. "We had to come with our guns literally blazing. That's what you are hearing. The maneuver is still in progress."

No pulse. Her sister had no pulse.

Grey froze in the corridor knowing she was hyperventilating, but she couldn't control it. "Rin's dead," she moaned. "She's dead."

"Grey, look at me."

"I can't lose her. I can't." She clamped onto her head with both hands, nearly crazed with dread. She'd never forget seeing her sister lying there on the floor. How could she possibly live without Rin?

Mrs. March placed her hands over Grey's. "Lord Jesus, we need a miracle. Please bring Rin back to us. We love her, and we need her. You are mighty and able. I trust you to take care of her." She gently lifted Grey's face. "And I pray for your peace to surround this dear girl right now. May she know it fully."

A group of Yien soldiers ran past, and Grey tried to focus on them. She knew she was endangering both herself and Mrs. March by breaking down. She had to get control of herself and allow Mrs. March to lead her to safety.

"I promised I'd protect her," she whispered.

"Our doctors have some wonderful technologies, Grey. They will help her. And we need to get you looked at too."

They ran through the central room with the now-empty cells, and Grey slowed when she saw several Mazdaar guards fallen on the concrete, their foreheads scorched and bloody from the beams that took their lives.

When they finally made it outside, darkness cloaked the Jupiter landscape. All that remained of the giant cosmoship *Genesis* was a pile of burning rubble.

More bodies littered the ground out here, and a wave of sorrow hit Grey. How many of these men and women had been pawns like Lee?

The landing lights of two new cosmoships, at least as large as *Genesis* had been, illuminated what looked like hundreds of Yien soldiers marching in formation and escorting members of the Mazdaar military who had been stripped of their armor. Other Yien soldiers were huddled over bodies, probably checking for survivors.

Mrs. March steered her toward the larger of the cosmoships as a man in black approached them. He wore the same

Yien armor as the others, but on his chest were six gold stars blazing in the waning light. She gawked when she saw his face.

Jet Yien bowed when he reached them.

Grey's eyes filled with tears. He'd tried to protect her from the beginning, and she hadn't trusted him.

"They have taken Rin to the ship's med bay," Jet said with a nod to Mrs. March. "I will escort Grey to her."

40

Grey and Jet walked approached the cargo doors of the huge Yien cosmoship. Soldiers were everywhere, and as a group of them trotted past, cool air whooshed across her still-swollen face.

"We have the very best doctors and medical equipment," Jet said, echoing Mrs. March. "Your mother is with her, and the doctors are working on her now."

"Did they bring her back?"

"I do not know. But come." He rested his strong arm across her back.

Why had Rin tried to take on the general by herself? If she had just waited for Grey to grab the laser, they might be standing beside each other now.

She tried to keep step with Jet and concentrated on his footsteps so she wouldn't break down again.

"Are you in pain?"

"I'm fine."

"I'm sorry we could not spare you this."

When they arrived at the med room, the odor hit Grey like a fog. Burnt and bloody men and women lay on cots scattered everywhere. Not all of them were Yien soldiers either. As she passed a bed where a young man with a bandaged head rested, she spotted the Mazdaar star on his green uniform.

Jet ushered her past the wounded and brought her into one of the private examination cubicles. "Let them check you."

"But—"

Jet disappeared behind the curtain, and Grey felt trapped again. She couldn't be alone. Not now.

She turned around as a white-haired man clad in scrubs entered from the other side. Grey's hand flew to her mouth.

"Dr. Lenoir!"

His sunken eyes widened. "Grey?"

"I thought you were dead."

"I almost was."

"Tessa?"

"She wanted you to live," Dr. Lenoir whispered. "I'm glad you did."

A grief she hadn't expected pushed up Grey's chest. "I'm sorry," she said, knowing it could never come close to expressing what she felt.

Dr. Lenoir cleared his throat and approached her as a doctor his patient, motioning for her to sit on the examination table bolted to the floor. She obeyed, wondering how he'd talked the Yien forces into allowing him to treat the wounded.

"I helped them deactivate the Mazdaar drones," Dr. Lenoir said, as if guessing her thoughts.

When Jet returned a few minutes later, her arm was re-bandaged, her facial cuts cleansed and dressed, and Dr. Lenoir had confirmed that the MI pistol hadn't caused her heart any permanent damage.

Grey flew to her feet when she saw Jet.

"Your sister is alive," he said.

Without thinking, Grey rushed over and gave Jet a hug. When it hit her that she was hugging royalty, she quickly pulled away, muttering apologies.

Jet laughed.

"How is she?" Grey asked, warmth rushing to her cheeks.

"Our doctors were able to revive her, but she has suffered several broken ribs, a cracked sternum, and a collapsed lung. The light therapist is with her now."

"What about my mom?"

"She took some hard blows too, but she'll be okay. She is quite remarkable." Jet smiled. "Just like her daughters."

When Grey crept up to her sister's cot, Rin lay deathly still under a blue sheet. A clear, oxygen halo shrouded her head. Grey dropped in a chair beside the bed and gently took Rin's hand. It was warm.

Rin's eyelids slowly opened.

"Hey." Grey sniffed and stroked her sister's hand.

"What . . . happened?" Rin's voice was faint and scratchy.

"You tried to take down a Mazdaar general," Grey said.

Rin reached out and touched Grey's battered face.

"I'm okay," Grey said.

Her sister knit her eyebrows.

"Really, kid. I am. But I don't know what I would've done if . . ." Grey gave Rin's hand a squeeze. "But we're here. We're both alive. And on Jupiter, no less." She tried to laugh, but it ended up coming out a choking sob. She dropped her head to the sheet as Rin drifted back to sleep. Yes, they were alive, but their lives were never going to be the same.

Later, when Rin woke up again and asked about Mom and Dad, Grey had to tell her they didn't know where Dad was. Was he buried under the rubble from the explosions?

She gave Rin a sip of water and helped her get more comfortable on her pillows.

"Grey?"

"Yeah?"

"Can you pray?"

She looked down at her little sister's hopeful face. Rin was the one who'd believed and kept the faith all these years. She was the one who could remember the verses and who stared up at the stars and talked about a Creator.

Grey started to say no like she always did, but something stopped her. She had to at least try. For Rin. She turned her gaze away and focused on the sterile floor. It took her a while to begin, but the words flowed from her tongue more easily than she imagined they would.

"Where can I go from your Spirit?" she began in a whisper. "Where can I flee from your presence? If I go up to the heavens, you are there." Grey thought of the millions of miles they'd traveled to get to this foreign planet. To God, the distance was probably nothing.

"If I make my bed in the depths, you are there," Grey continued. "If I rise on the wings of the dawn, if I settle on the far side of the sea, even there your hand will guide me, your right hand will hold me fast."

She paused, trying to remember the next phrase. She could've been killed multiple times since setting foot on Jupiter's surface, yet somehow she'd survived.

"If I say, 'Surely, the darkness will hide me and the light become night around me,' even the darkness will not be dark to you; the night will shine like the day, for darkness is as light to you."

Grey knew it wasn't really a prayer, but Rin didn't seem to mind. She practically beamed. Then Grey felt a hand on her shoulder and looked up into her mother's black-and-blue face.

How long had she been standing there?
Mom was smiling too.

Grey slept on the floor beside Rin's hospital bed that night. Her sister's injuries would heal, but the doctors told them it would take a few weeks before she was completely back on her feet.

When Grey awoke in the morning, at first she thought she was back in the silo. Quickly coming back to reality, she wondered if she'd ever see the silo again. She slipped from the room, careful not to wake her sister, and found her way outside.

Another ten-hour day had dawned on Jupiter, and Yien forces bustled around the landing site. Sentinels guarded supplies while others patrolled the perimeter with finely-tuned ocelli and auris implants, ready to detect the slightest threat.

Jet said yesterday that some Yien drones were being used, though all of Mazdaar's drones, had been captured and deactivated. After reprogramming, they too could eventually be utilized to defend the settlement and would build the Yien forces up to almost a thousand, though Dr. Lenoir would make sure his son-in-law's body got a proper burial.

Grey ended up outside the animal pens. A smile came to her lips when she laid eyes on the zorses.

"Hey, boys."

A soft nicker came from the pen. Grey let herself inside the makeshift gate, and they surrounded her and pressed their noses into her palms looking for treats. She stroked their necks and scratched their withers. What really remained for her back on Earth anyway? She'd miss the only home she'd ever known, but her family was here. Except for Dad. He hadn't been among the prisoners or the dead. It was like he'd disappeared into thin air. Again.

Grey firmly rubbed the inside of Tram's ear, and he turned his head to lean into it. She was glad Rin had managed to bring the animals. Grey always tried to keep herself from getting attached, but the zorses had wriggled into her family anyway.

When she heard shouts, at first she thought it was just part of a routine military drill. But her mother came rushing over, gesturing wildly.

She jumped out of the pen. "What's going on?"

"There's an alert." Mom ushered her at a run back toward the cosmoship as Mrs. March and several armed guards poured from the cargo doors. The commander was pointing toward the trees.

Grey strained to make out two figures emerging from behind the contorted trunks. One of them was Yurkutz's daughter, Dana.

The other was Dad.

As they approached, Grey saw that Dana held a violetflare to her father's head. His arms were tied behind his back, no doubt with shock cuffs.

"Hold your fire!" Mrs. March yelled.

Grey looked at Mom. Her back had gone rigid.

"Oh, Dana, why?" Mom whispered.

"Call them off!"

When Mrs. March hesitated, Dana must've activated the cuffs. Dad suddenly doubled over.

"I said call them off!"

Commander March ordered everyone to pull back, but the Yien soldiers kept their weapons trained on the pair steadily moving closer.

"Release Tanner and surrender yourself, Dana," Mrs. March said with authority. "We will not hurt you."

"Where is my mother?"

So that was it. She wanted Yurkutz.

"She is alive and in our custody." Mrs. March edged closer. "Dana, please. You don't need to do this. We will be merciful."

"I'm not negotiating." Dana pushed Dad forward again, the laser gun still jammed into his temple. "You will release my mother to me, and only then will I give you Tanner."

"You know we can't do that."

"Then I'll kill him."

Grey felt herself tense. Hadn't her parents rescued this girl from Mazdaar? Why had she turned on them?

"Dana, be reasonable. It's over." Mrs. March was probably twenty feet away from them now, steadily inching closer. "You are outnumbered. If you kill Tanner, you will be shot immediately."

"Stay back!"

Mrs. March stopped in her tracks.

"You think I'm not serious?" Dana yelled.

"I can see you are."

"You never convinced me with all your religion and corny love of freedom." Dana's face looked flushed, her hair sweaty and sticking to her forehead. "Mazdaar is the greatest thing that ever happened to Earth and now to Jupiter, and all you want to do is ruin it."

"Honey, Mazdaar is not taking Jupiter."

"But you are?" Dana laughed as if trying to sound relaxed, like she was in control. She shoved the gun harder against Dad's head, and he flinched. "There's only one way out of this, *Commander*. Release my mother and swear to me by the god you serve that you won't follow us."

Grey watched Mrs. March's back rise and fall. Then she waved one of her men over and said something in his ear. He rushed off toward the cosmoship.

"I will give her to you, Dana."

Mrs. March took a step closer. Dana didn't seem to notice. "Do you have any idea what your mother was planning to do here?"

"You'll provide us one of your Jeeps too." Grey could see Dana was breathing heavily.

"Commander, don't consider me." Dad's voice was weak, but his words sliced through Grey.

"I most certainly will," Mrs. March said.

Within a few moments, a bound Evangeline Yurkutz was led from the cosmoship by four Yien guards. Grey was surprised to recognize Kildare Rooley among them. She hadn't realized he was a Yien operative.

Yurkutz was limping heavily, but her back remained as erect as ever. They walked her right past Grey. She closed her eyes and didn't realize she was squeezing Mom's hand in a death grip until her mother gently loosened her fingers with her own. She could not believe this was happening.

The guards led Yurkutz over to Mrs. March.

"Undo her restraints," Dana said.

"Release Tanner first."

"Not until you untie my mother."

Mrs. March's lips pursed. "Release Tanner! I have given you my word. You know full well I will keep it."

Dana looked at her mother then back to Mrs. March. She slowly released Dad with one hand while still holding the violetflare on him. She pushed him toward Mrs. March, taking a step backward. Mrs. March quickly grabbed his arm to steady him and gestured to the guards. They hesitated, but they cut the plastic tie-cuffs from the general's wrists.

Why didn't Mrs. March just shoot them both while she could? They certainly deserved it.

Even hobbling, Yurkutz looked defiant as she walked over to her daughter.

Another Yien soldier drove an old Jeep over to Dana and quickly jumped out, leaving it running. Dana leveled her laser in Mrs. March's direction while she and her mother climbed in.

"How can she just release them?" Grey heard her voice rising.

"I don't know, but I trust her," Mom whispered.

As Dana helped her mother into the Jeep, Yurkutz glanced back. Of all the people standing in that crowd, of all the faces, she made eye contact with Grey. Then the Jeep shot forward across the Jupiter landscape and past the dumbfounded Yien soldiers who helplessly watched, their guns still raised and ready to open fire.

As soon as the Jeep was out of sight, Mom ran across the clearing to Dad, Grey right behind her. One of the guards cut off Dad's restraints.

Her parents embraced, and five years of longing turned to joy. They held each other, tears streaming down both of their faces.

"Where were you?" Mom whispered. "We searched for weeks after the crash."

He kissed her forehead. "I hit the surface hard. I think I was out for two days. When I woke up, I couldn't find you or the crew. I thought you all were dead. If I hadn't found a group of refugees that took me, I would be too."

He kept hold of Mom but opened his arms to Grey. "Come here, kiddo."

Grey fell into his embrace too.

"Look at you," he said. "So tall and pretty."

She leaned into his chest. "I missed you, Daddy."

Finally, all three of them turned to Mrs. March. Her father explained how right after the first explosions hit the dome and the Mazdaar soldiers were in a panic Dana had taken him from his cell, out an underground exit, and into the woods.

"Where's Rinny?" he asked.

Grey told him, and he insisted on going straight to see her. He still looked pale from the macro-shocks he'd received, and she and Mom had to support him under the arms as they slowly walked toward the cosmoship together.

They started up the cargo ramp, but not before Grey noticed Mrs. March huddle with several of the Yien guards beside the ship. She was obviously giving orders, and they were intently listening.

"I'll meet you inside," Grey said to her parents, then headed straight for her former neighbor.

Mrs. March turned as she approached.

"Why did you let her go?" Grey waved in the direction of the Jeep. "After what she's done?"

Mrs. March gave her a tight smile. "We're not done with Evangeline. I had to give her to Dana to save your father, but I specifically did not promise her we wouldn't follow them." Mrs. March tried to usher Grey up into the ship. "But this is not something you need to worry about, dear. Your family needs you. Go enjoy them."

Grey wanted to obey her and revel in her reunited family, but she knew she could never fully enjoy it knowing General Yurkutz was still out there. As long as she was alive, her family would always be in danger.

She jutted out her chin. "If you're following them, I'm going with you."

"No, you're not."

Grey stood her ground while trying to remain respectful. "Mrs. March, you taught me how to survive in the Preserve.

You trusted me to get information to your operatives. I always came back safely, even when the odds were against me."

"Yes, and every time I worried like a mother hen. If something had happened to you I would never have forgiven myself. Grey, you have done well. Now your family needs you."

She followed Mrs. March up the ramp. "So do you and Jet. You know I'm a good tracker. I can help."

Mrs. March rolled her eyes, throwing her hands in the air. "Oh, Lord, when will I learn how persistent an Alexander can be?"

Grey followed her to the ship's armory in silence, knowing better than to push too far. The compact space was filled with rifles, graphene body suits, and even a mechanical robot "ox" for use in the field to carry heavy equipment.

"I will allow you to go on three conditions," Mrs. March finally said. "One, your parents must agree." She ticked off a finger. "Two, you will not engage Evangeline or Dana in any way."

Grey was already nodding, mentally calculating how far they could've gotten by now. That Jeep was certainly capable of speed, but the terrain would slow them down considerably. How much fuel did it have?

"And three, I will accompany you."

"What?"

"A large party will draw attention. I had already decided to send only two. And you are right." Mrs. March smiled. "You are a good tracker."

Her parents were harder to convince, but when Grey assured them she'd be with Mrs. March the whole time, they consented, though it was hard to forget the look of sad resignation on her mother's face.

Ten minutes later, Grey had Tram and Trif tacked up and ready to go. She handed Mrs. March Trif's reins and led Tram out of the pen.

"Have you ridden before?" Grey asked.

Mrs. March laughed. "You really don't know me, do you?"

"And whose fault is that?" Grey said it with a grin, but a small part of her wished she'd been old enough for these Yien officers to trust her and Rin with their secrets back in the Preserve. Maybe it had protected them not to know, but she felt like she was only now meeting the real Mrs. March, the same way she'd only just met her real parents.

They mounted and rode off without fanfare. Commander March would keep in contact with Jet and the base via a radio plug in her ear. Until Yien could get satellites orbiting, everyone would have to rely on old-fashioned methods for long-range communications. To the connected it would feel backwards, but Grey didn't have any trouble adapting.

She had opted to ride with a removable ocelli implant like the one she'd used back home. It didn't require the long distance signals other equipment needed, and she could activate it with a bracelet controller just like her old one.

Side by side on the zorses, a pang of longing for the Preserve hit her.

"Can we ever go back home?" Grey asked.

"Do you want to?"

She urged Tram into a trot with a small squeeze of her calves. "I'm not sure."

"When we took off, they were bombing the Preserve," Mrs. March said. "I don't know how much is even left."

"The silo?"

"You would never be safe there again."

Regret washed over her. The only home she'd ever known

was gone, probably destroyed. Grey stared at the distorted Jupiter trees, the swirling orange clouds and multi-colored dirt. There was a beauty here she couldn't deny, but Earth was still in her blood.

"What do we do when we find them?" Grey felt herself relaxing on Tram's familiar back.

"We need to track where they go." Mrs. March kept up on Trif, seemingly as at ease on a zorse as she was in a cockpit. "That's it."

"I don't understand why we don't just capture them."

"I gave my word."

"But this is war. That's different."

"To some."

Grey and Mrs. March followed the Jeep's tracks easily in the powdery soil. The tracks showed that Dana had had to drive around the forest since the space between the trees wouldn't allow for a vehicle that size.

"We should cut through the woods," Grey said. "We'll shave off time."

Mrs. March nodded. "Lead on."

"Give Trif free rein, and he'll follow me." Grey touched Tram's sides with her heels. "Go, boy!"

He immediately jumped into a lope, dashing through the trees. She gave him his head and trusted him to carry her through the forest without smacking her into any branches. She could hear Trif's hooves following close behind. At this rate, they might be able to cut the pair off on the other side.

Mrs. March had given Grey strict orders not to engage, and she'd learned her lesson about going rogue. She wasn't risking Mrs. March's life on an impulse for revenge, though fire still burned inside her when she thought about seeing Yurkutz again, even at a distance.

They wove their way through the trees, slowing to cross a

stream that shimmered like silver. This must be the water Mom had talked about, the stuff that fueled the lanterns. As they passed through the shallow water, Tram spooked at a huge shadowy figure under the surface that looked like the biggest scorpion Grey had ever seen. It darted away before she could even ask Mrs. March what it was.

As the trees thinned and Grey could see the sky in front of them, she slowed Tram to a walk, and Mrs. March mirrored her on Trif. The zorses were sweating and breathing hard, but she knew they loved the exercise. They were happiest when they were doing something. Just like her.

"How can anyone be so evil?" Grey whispered.

"She is deceived."

Grey pulled up gently on her reins before they left the safety of the forest. She dismounted, tying Tram to one of the low-hanging branches. Mrs. March did the same with Trif.

Grey tapped at her bracelet controller, switching to the ocelli's panoramic view. She hoped they'd arrived in time to beat the Jeep.

"See anything?" Mrs. March asked.

"Maybe." Grey crept toward the clearing. There were now only a few trunks protecting her from view. They had to tread carefully from here.

She scanned the meadow with the curly, angel-hair grass in front of them and the buttes beyond. They probably weren't far from Mom's old camp now. Grey pointed to an object on the edge of the woods about a hundred yards to their left. "There."

It was the Jeep.

Grey zoomed in on the Jeep with the ocelli, but she saw no signs of General Yurkutz or Dana. Had they abandoned the vehicle or ran out of fuel? Maybe they'd tried to push through the brush and the tires had gotten caught on something.

"Wait," Mrs. March mouthed, and Grey agreed with a quick nod. They needed to make sure Dana and her mother were definitely no longer in the area before they approached.

After staking it out for fifteen minutes, they were convinced the Mazdaar women had deserted the vehicle. Grey carefully picked her way through the trees toward the Jeep, Mrs. March right beside her. Each of them now firmly held the blueflare rifles they'd slung across their backs while riding.

How far could Dana and her wounded mother possibly have gone? Jupiter's night would be coming in just a few hours, and they'd have to travel between lightning flashes or take cover somewhere safe in the forest before the winds came again and the animals began hunting. Grey got more nervous with each step toward the Jeep. If they were on foot, she and Mrs. March could catch up with them on Tram and Trif. Maybe she could talk Mrs. March into taking the women as prisoners after all.

She glided the final yards through the trees to the vehicle. Mrs. March signaled for Grey to approach from the passenger side while she approached the driver's side. A quick check confirmed the Jeep was empty.

Mrs. March opened the door and seemed to be checking the vehicle's gauges. "That doesn't make sense."

"What?" Grey peered inside too.

"The fuel gauge says there's still half a tank."

"They broke down?"

"These vehicles were in pristine condition," Mrs. March said.

Examining the tires, which showed no signs of damage, Grey had to agree there didn't seem to be anything wrong on the outside of the Jeep. But she knew nothing of autos. Pristine or not, something as old as this could break at any time, right? Standing side-by-side, their backs to the forest, they stared at the vehicle.

"What should we do?"

A sickening thud answered her, and Mrs. March dropped to the ground.

Grey whirled to see Dana poised over the commander, a branch the size of her arm raised and ready to strike again.

"No! Stop!" Grey aimed her rifle.

Laser fire sizzled through the air, and before Grey could pull the trigger the rifle flew from her hands, its muzzle twisted into a gnarled, smoking hunk of metal.

The Mazdaar general limped from the trees, aiming a violetflare straight at Grey's heart.

"What did I tell you?" Yurkutz called to her daughter. "I knew they'd follow us."

Dana still had her club raised but didn't strike Mrs. March again. Had she killed her? No. Grey saw the old woman's hand twitch.

Yurkutz pursed her lips. "How many others are coming?"

Grey thought about lying and promising a whole squadron was right behind them, but she didn't know if that would make this better or worse.

At her silence, the woman swung the weapon toward Mrs. March. "I said how many others?"

"None," Grey muttered.

The Mazdaar general's yellow eyes narrowed.

"It's just us."

"I don't believe you."

She shrugged, trying to pretend she didn't care. Was this how it was all going to end? After escaping the general's grasp the first time, was she going to die at her hand now?

Grey tried to stay calm. She had just been reunited with her family. She should've listened to Mrs. March and stayed with them. They needed her, and now she wasn't going to be able to help them at all.

"Tie her up," Yurkutz ordered her daughter with a nod at Mrs. March's still form. "I saw some rope in the back of the Jeep."

Grey knew better than to try and fight them both. Even with Yurkutz's wounded leg, the two would overpower her, and she'd be putting Mrs. March's life at risk. It was better to wait.

Dana flipped Mrs. March onto her back, roughly wrapping rope around her hands. She tied the woman's ankles too, cinching the rope tight. It was all Grey could do to keep from punching Dana.

"What are you going to do with her?"

With a chuckle, Yurkutz hobbled closer. "And I thought *you* were valuable." She kicked at Mrs. March's foot. "Help Dana put her in the Jeep. If you try anything, I will kill her and enjoy it."

Grey moved toward Mrs. March. If she grabbed the old woman's radio, could she transmit something before they noticed? Grey scooped Mrs. March up in her arms by herself. At least she could carry her gently over to the Jeep.

Mrs. March moaned as she placed her on the back seat.

"It'll be okay," Grey whispered, her fingers brushing the radio plug. Before she could grab it, Dana yanked her away from Mrs. March, and for a second the two girls faced each other.

If it had been just the two of them, Grey would've fought without hesitation. But she'd be no good to Mrs. March dead, and that's exactly what she'd be if she struck Yurkutz's daughter.

Grey backed away from the auto, facing Yurkutz again. The Mazdaar general's normally-spiked hair lay flat on her head, dried blood clumping the strands on her temple.

"You can kill me, but you're still not gonna win," Grey said softly, suddenly catching a whiff of an iron-tinged smell that somehow seemed familiar.

Yurkutz raised the violetflare. "Neither are you, Alexander."

"Wait, what are you doing?" Dana stepped forward. "We got March; that's what you wanted."

Shaking her head, Yurkutz shifted off her wounded leg. "No one crosses me and lives. Or have you forgotten that too?"

The metallic scent grew stronger. Grey had smelled it before, but where? Certainly not here on Jupiter.

"But you said we'd keep them both alive!" Dana glanced at Grey with bloodshot eyes.

The corner of the general's mouth twisted. "I lied."

She swung the laser back to Grey, straightening her arm. And Grey knew it was over. There was no one to rescue her this time. She was going to die.

I'm yours now, God. I guess I always have been, haven't I?

"Mother, no!"

The barrel of the weapon flashed just as Dana threw herself between Grey and Yurkutz. Laser beam met flesh, and Dana fell to the mossy forest floor and lay still.

Grey froze, taking in her fallen body. Was she dead?

Yurkutz stepped over to her daughter and knelt down, and the metallic odor wafted to Grey's nose again, only stronger. She remembered where she'd smelled it before. Grey surreptitiously brushed her bracelet controller with her finger, and the ocelli responded instantly.

She scanned the trees and spotted a flash of orange fur. But Mazdaar General Evangeline Yurkutz did not. As she stood and aimed to fire again at Grey, a low growl reverberated through the trees. Yurkutz's eyes flicked to the side a moment too late as the tiger lunged from behind its cover of brush. Her eyes widened in terror as the tiger leapt at her. The general collapsed to the ground under the massive animal's body, and with one snap of its jaws, her scream cut off in a gurgle.

Grey reached down and picked up Yurkutz's weapon. She carefully backed away, her eyes never leaving the gigantic feline. It stood over Yurkutz in triumph, paws planted on her chest.

Slowly, Grey dropped down and pressed her fingers to Dana's wrist, surprised to feel a faint pulse. The tiger's ears twitched, and it backed off Yurkutz's body and lay down beside her.

That's when Kildare Rooley emerged from the trees.

Kildare gave Grey a slight nod, but she could only stare at the lifeless body of the Mazdaar general.

44

"Y ou sure you're up for this?" Grey supported Rin, helping her navigate the cosmoship's narrow corridor.

"You don't exactly say no to the emperor's son," Rin said.

"He'd understand."

"I'm fine, Grey."

"You shouldn't even be out of bed."

Her little sister smiled up at her. "You know I'm never letting you out of my sight again, right?"

Grey patted Rin on the head as if she was five, and her sister ducked out from under her, laughing. For the first time since arriving on Jupiter everything felt right, and Grey allowed herself to just enjoy being with her sister again. Rin was safe. Mom and Dad were alive, and so was Mrs. March. She'd suffered a mild concussion from Dana's blow but was already back to work against doctor's orders.

Dana hadn't been so lucky. She was still hanging on to life this morning but lay unconscious in the intensive care unit.

Grey might never know why, after her traitorous defection from Mrs. March, she had tried to save her. Rin had spent an hour by the girl's bedside this morning, even though she herself was still weak.

"Tram and Trif are okay?" Rin asked.

Grey smiled. "I checked them this morning. I think they might be happier here than they were at home. The air seems to invigorate them." She couldn't wait to show Rin the orphaned Tasmanian wolf cub Kildare's son Jonah had found.

At the entrance to Jet's personal chamber, Grey and Rin paused. A Yien drone saluted them, and Grey forced herself to return it. She'd never get used to drones, but at least she could be sure these were purely machines.

The size of the chamber caught her by surprise. It was almost as large as the entire lounge on *Genesis*. Jet had even placed what looked like live, exotic plants in massive pots along the perimeter. How had these withstood the rigors of flight?

In the middle of the room was a circular table burgeoning with food. Grey took in a long whiff, and her mouth started watering.

"Oh my word." Rin's eyes widened. "Look at the size of those strawberries."

Grey had already spotted them, along with the wedges of dark chocolate, slices of kiwi, and a plate of a dozen kinds of cheese.

Jet approached them from across the room, bowing like always. "Might I interest you in some refreshment?"

They couldn't help the huge smiles that instantly came to their faces.

Jet chuckled. "I take that as a yes? Please be seated."

Grey reminded herself to be polite and not dive into the food.

It had been so different when she'd thought of Jet as a

wealthy Mazdaar socialite. Now she was finding herself nervous in his presence.

"Do not wait on my account, ladies," Jet said.

"Thank you," they both said in unison. Grey reached for the cheese; Rin grabbed a strawberry and took a huge bite. The juice dripped down her chin and she giggled, quickly dabbing it away with a cloth napkin.

Grey smiled. She loved hearing Rin actually laugh like a fourteen-year-old girl again.

"I hope you are feeling better," Jet said to Rin.

"Still sore," she said.

His brow furrowed. "And you, Grey?"

"I'll live."

Jet sat down, folding his hands on the table. "I thought it fitting to invite the two of you up here first. Just like old times, correct? You have helped us immensely these past few years, and we are extremely grateful."

Grey nodded, stuffing a hunk of nutty bread into her mouth and elbowing Rin to pay attention. She could hardly blame her for staring around the room. The walls were lined with what looked like real wood panels carved with delicate images of Earth's trees, animals, and mountains.

"Let me show you something." Jet leapt to his feet again, rushing over to the nearest wall, his black tailcoat swirling around him. He pressed his thumb on an invisible sensor and the wall slid back, revealing an alcove lined with bookshelves.

Grey stood too, walking over to it. Crowded onto the shelves were books of every shape, size, and color. A few were even bound in leather. Rin followed Grey, and they gawked at the ancient volumes. It would take a lifetime to read all of them.

"Beautiful?" Jet gestured at the books with a dramatic flourish.

"Where did you get these?"

"Actually, you helped me acquire many of them." He pulled a title off the shelf and handed it to her. "Remember this?"

Apology by Plato. One of the books they'd sold him on that last mission on Earth. Grey carefully took it and held it in her hands.

"Mankind is doomed if we lose our history." Jet turned somber. "If we are to begin anew on Jupiter, we must not forget where we came from. That is why I have brought these here. You cannot delete a paper book except with fire, and we will make sure that does not happen."

Grey handed the Plato back to him. "This is amazing."

Jet smiled as he oversaw the collection.

Grey returned to the table with her sister, eying a pastry smothered in white glaze and slivered almonds. "But surely you didn't summon us here just for a good meal."

"This is somewhat of a celebration." Jet nodded toward the door.

They turned to see Mrs. March, Mom, Dad, and several other Yien leaders enter the quarters.

"First, I would like to announce that we have successfully seized Orion settlement," Jet said. "Our next objective is to secure the others in order of proximity." A map as large as he materialized in the air beside him. Jet indicated several points in quick succession. "These are the remaining Mazdaar settlements."

"There are more?" Grey squinted to read the coordinates.

Mom nodded, looking every bit the part of Captain Sue Alexander. She'd changed into a starched, black uniform shirt and new canvas pants. The bandage on her temple added to her battle-worn image. She'd been on the front lines and come through.

"Two years ago, one of my scouts was captured and taken to this one." Mom pointed to a spot on the map. "We were never able to penetrate it."

Dad stood proudly beside his wife, his civilian clothes clean and pressed. This morning, Grey had finally heard the whole story of what happened to him after he and Mom were separated. He had hit the surface a thousand kilometers from Orion settlement and spent a year completely alone. Finally, he found a group of former Mazdaar convicts who allowed him to stay with them for a few years. When they were able to salvage enough parts to construct a transceiver, he learned that Mazdaar was looking for him on Jupiter. He started picking up broadcasts demanding he turn himself in. It was only when one transmission said Mazdaar had captured Grey that Dad felt he had to respond.

Jet waved his hand, and the map switched to a survey of Earth. He zoomed in on North America. Several bright, red dots were scattered across the continent. "We have over two hundred Yien military cosmoships like this one on their way now."

Mrs. March stepped forward. "And forty-eight more like the one in the Alexander's silo, all carrying civilians."

Grey started to ask something but then stopped herself. She and Rin were lucky to even be allowed in this room.

Jet turned toward Grey. "Please feel free to speak."

She cleared her throat. "Once Mazdaar realizes what you've done, won't they launch an attack to stop you and send for reinforcements?"

The room went silent.

"They already have," Jet finally said. "They are on their way too."

Which could only mean one thing—they were at war. Grey watched Mrs. March studying the map with her comrades. She was the first person who had tried to explain the importance of Jupiter to her back in the Preserve a lifetime ago. Grey was beginning to understand its significance. The Yien Dynasty wanted to give humankind a chance at the freedom they'd lost on Earth. But Grey knew breaking free from oppression never came without a price. More people would die.

She looked at her parents, then at Rin. Grey could've lost everything. Instead, she'd gained more than she could have ever hoped to. She knew Who to thank for that.

"There will be many battles," Mrs. March said. "Mazdaar won't give up easily; we're sure of that."

"Why do they want Jupiter?" Grey asked. "They already have most of Earth."

Jet waved his hand in response. "Why did the great monarchs yearn to reach the ends of the world and the great outer sea? It is the nature of empires to conquer. My father is no exception, but we conquer to protect our subjects, not to enslave them."

"How long before *our* reinforcements arrive?"

"A day at most," Mrs. March said as she came closer to Grey and Rin. A goose-egg of a lump marred her forehead near the hairline, no doubt from the blow she'd sustained from Dana.

"However, we brought you in here for more than a briefing," Mrs. March said. "We are here to officially commend both of you."

"But I haven't done anything," Grey said. "Rin has, but I—"

"That is not true." Mrs. March took one of Grey's hands, looking her in the eyes. "I have watched you ever since you were born. Your bravery, honesty, and loyalty are qualities we admire.

"You willingly put yourself in harm's way numerous times

to provide for your sister. And you allowed yourself to be captured to protect her. You also helped protect me."

And she would do it all again in a heartbeat.

"Bravery isn't always about wielding weapons," Mrs. March continued, "though I know you have done that too. Your mother told me how you were willing to sacrifice yourself to save the prisoners here."

The corners of the elderly commander's mouth turned up. "We need more like you, Grey Alexander, which is why we are asking you to enlist."

She glanced at her parents, who both gave her nods of affirmation.

Jet stepped forward. "We do not conscript in the Yien Dynasty. It is your choice. And if you decide against it, you will in no way be diminished in our eyes."

Grey felt flustered, completely taken off guard at the invitation. It surprised her that anyone would want her to enlist after how she'd almost gotten herself and her mother killed yesterday. And no matter what Mrs. March said, she didn't feel brave. She did what she had to do. That was it. Bravery belonged to someone like Rin, who'd tried to subdue a Mazdaar general, or to Dad for destroying his chip research to save lives, or to Mom for commandeering an entire refugee camp on a foreign planet for five years.

"I don't really know why you'd want me," she said. "But if you'll have me, I'll happily join."

Everyone clapped, including Rin, and Grey managed a smile.

"We are honored, Specialist Alexander," Jet said, giving her a bow.

"Wait . . . what?"

Mrs. March chuckled. "That is your rank, dear." She turned toward Rin. "And you, Orinda. You have shown yourself to be quite valuable these past few days. You will have great potential in a few years."

Rin flushed, and Grey was glad her little sister was getting recognition too.

"Your devotion to your family is precious and will never be forgotten. Your love for your sister drove you to make sacrifices and forego your own safety on more than one occasion. You are too young for us to ask you to enlist. But we look forward to working with you in a few years. You will be a rock others can lean upon."

"I . . ." Rin stared at the floor. "I'll do my best."

Mrs. March reached out and gave Rin a hug. "You are more special than you realize. Someday I hope you will know it." There was more applause as the sisters looked at each other.

Grey could feel herself blushing uncomfortably. But when Mom whispered in her ear how proud she was, nothing else mattered.

AUTHOR'S NOTE:

If you enjoyed this story, I'd love it if you would leave a short review on some of the online sites like Amazon, B&N, and Goodreads. Every review helps! Thank you.

You can always feel free to e-mail me at: cj@cjdarlington.com

For the very latest on my books, join my mailing list through this link: http://www.tinyurl.com/cjdarlingtonlist

ABOUT THE AUTHOR

C. J. Darlington is the award-winning author of the contemporary novels *Thicker than Blood, Bound by Guilt,* and *Ties that Bind.* She is a co-founder of Mountainview Books, LLC and makes her home in Pennsylvania with her family and their menagerie of animals.

Visit her website at www.cjdarlington.com

DISCUSSION QUESTIONS
Warning: Spoilers ahead!

If your book club reads *Jupiter Winds* and is interested in talking with me via speakerphone or Skype, please feel free to contact me by email at cj@cjdarlington.com, and I'll do my best to arrange something with you. Thanks for reading, and you can always visit my website: www.cjdarlington.com for more info.

1. Why would someone not want to be "connected"?

2. What Biblical principle do you think is most prevalent in the story?

3. Do you think these same principles would apply on any planet?

4. What are your feelings about General Yurkutz? How do you think she became like she is?

5. Why do you think Grey has given up on prayer?

6. Do you agree with Tanner and Sue Alexander's decision to hide what they were doing from their children or not?

7. Which character did you most relate to and why?

8. What seeds can you see that Sue Alexander had sown into her daughters before she left?

9. If you could talk to Dana, what would you say? How do you think she should be treated by the Yien Dynasty and the Alexander family?

10. How could forgiveness be important in this story?

11. Who do you think experiences the most personal growth?

12. Do you believe God has other planets in the universe with life as we know it? Is there any Biblical reference for this?

13. What technology in *Jupiter Winds* do you think really could be in our future?

14. If you could resurrect any extinct animal on Earth, which would you pick and why?

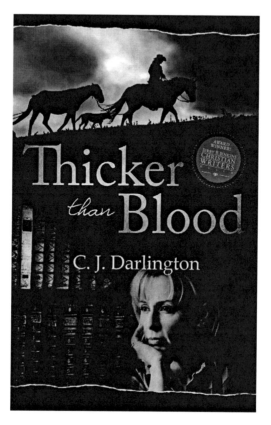

Two estranged sisters, one a rare book dealer, the other a cattle rancher, meet again after fifteen years.

Christy Williams finally has her life on track. She's putting her past behind her and working hard to build a career as an antiquarian book buyer. She could never imagine that a stolen first edition of *For Whom the Bell Tolls* would lead her back to the sister she abandoned fifteen years ago. With her life in danger, can May's Triple Cross Ranch be the safe haven Christy's searching for? Will the sisters realize before it's too late that each possesses what the other desperately needs?

**A botched robbery at a used bookstore sends a
guilt-ridden teen girl on the run.**

Foster kid Roxi Gold longs for a family and will do anything
to fit in—even if it's against the law. Police officer Abby
Dawson has seen the worst of society, and not just at work.
One fateful night a man's innocent blood changes both Roxi's
and Abby's lives forever. One searches for justice; the other
finds herself fleeing with a stolen first edition of *The Great
Gatsby*. Will the power of forgiveness set them free or will they
both remain bound by guilt?

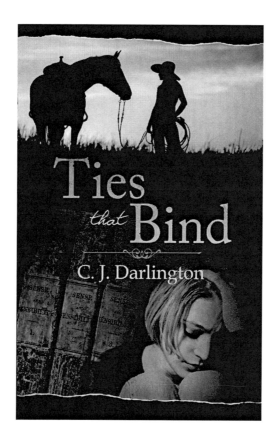

On a quest to find her father, a young woman discovers she has two sisters who have no idea she exists.

Newly released from prison, Brynn Taylor is determined to find her father, a man she's never met. Her only clue to his whereabouts is an address she finds in a rare volume of Jane Austen's *Sense & Sensibility* which he inscribed to her years ago. Armed with a bus ticket, a backpack, and her grandfather's gun, her search leads her to Elk Valley, Colorado where her plans and her life begin to unravel.

Visit the Mountainview Books, LLC website for news on all our books:

www.mountainviewbooks.com

CPSIA information can be obtained at www.ICGtesting.com
Printed in the USA
BVOW07s0003061114

373862BV00004B/244/P